COME ADVENTURING WITH ME!

# The Secret of

# O*A*K

# I*S*L*A*ND

*A Juvenile Mystery-Adventure Story*

*by Bertram Smith*

# The Author's Note

*This story was written in 1963 through the eyes of the brilliant, hilarious, adventurous imagination of the author:*

*Mr. Bertram Smith.*

*The manuscript was never published and tucked away, long forgotten, only to be rediscovered in the family attic in 2022 by his granddaughter, Pamdiana Jones*

*Already an adventure author in her own right, and already fascinated by the 200-year long true history of the Oak Island Treasure Hunt, Pamdiana Jones decided to type up this manuscript, word for word from that era, and hand it to her mother, triplet Wendy, as a gift for her 75th birthday.*

*Truly enjoy this fun, inspiring, exciting family's escapades.*

*Published by Turtle Publishing House*

*Copyright © 2023 Pamdiana Jones Turtle Publishing*

*ISBN: 978-1-7352736-2-4*

*Original Manuscript Author: Mr. Bertram Smith*

*Author: Pamdiana Jones*

*Cover Design: Jaycee DeLorenzo of Sweet 'N Spicy Designs*

# Contents.

# Chapter One

## *FLIGHT TO ADVENTURE.*

Harold Pallant strode into the kitchen thinking only of food after a busy morning of farm chores. He found his parents standing together, reading a letter.

"Harry!" exclaimed his father. "How would you like to spend a vacation on a schooner?"

The boy stopped in mid-stride and stared. His mouth opened and closed, but no sound came out. Then he gulped and managed, "A vacation on a schooner? What do you mean?"

Hi parents chuckled at the reaction. "This is a letter from your Uncle Fred," continued his father. "You remember he moved his family from Canada to Maine last year. Now he writes to tell us that he bought an old schooner. The whole family spent the winter refitting it, and they plan to sail up the coast soon. They wonder if you would like to go along."

"You haven't seen them since you were a baby," put in his mother, "Although we do have photos of them and their four children. Anita is the eldest – she must be grown by now. The triplets – Wendy, Pauline, and Peter are only a few months older than you, so you are all thirteen. What more could you ask?"

Harry was having difficulty in grasping all this. He sat down at the table mechanically, and his father joined him. "You lucky dog! You know your Uncle Fred and I were at sea together in our younger days. I sure wish I could go with you."

Now the boy was beginning to grasp the situation. "But what about the farm?" he began, but his father cut him short. "Don't worry about it. We'll manage somehow. This is the chance of a lifetime for you!"

"Of course it is," said his mother briskly. "When you've finished eating, we'll decide what clothes you will need, and then go do some shopping."

"Good idea," Mr. Pallant agreed. "While you are gone, I will make some inquiries about travel from here to Maine."

Harry ate automatically, his mind in a whirl. He had often read about adventures on schooners but had never dreamed that such a thing could possibly happen to him. After all, he had lived his whole life in Missouri and never even see the sea.

When they returned from the sopping trip, Harry's father met them with: "I telephoned your Uncle Fred and told him how thrilled we all are. They expect to set sail next week, but you are welcome to go as soon as you like. So, I booked you on the noon flight tomorrow on Continental Airlines! Allowing for the time change, you should arrive in Portland nicely in time for supper."

"Wonderful!" exclaimed Mrs. Pallant. "You'd better pack tonight, son. It's a sixty-mile drive to the airport, so you won't have much time for it tomorrow morning."

Harry sat down feeling a little dazed. So much had happened in these last few hours that he was having difficulty in keeping up with it all. However, the thought of packing made him realize that his was no dream, so he went up to his room to get started.

That night, he dreamt of sailing on a schooner in the South Seas. When he awoke, he found it difficult to believe that in a few hours, he would be taking his first airplane trip and, soon afterwards, his first sea voyage.

During the drive to the airport Harry began to think about flying. Despite reassurances from his parents, he was concerned about air sickness. It would be awful if his first flight was spoiled by that. Then maybe later he would have to worry about sea-sickness! Watching the familiar green fields slip by, he began to wonder if he really wanted to go.

The huge air terminal at Kansas City almost overwhelmed him with noise and bustle. It was crowded with people in a hurry and apparently ignoring the public address system which was blaring out continually. This was presumably intended to help them, but Harry found it impossible to understand what was being said.

Through the spacious windows, aircraft were visible taxying to and from the runways while, in the distance, others were taking off and landing. A plane with Continental Airlines emblazoned on its side taxied into view and the boy realized with a thrill that it might well be the one he was to travel on.

The ticket line-up moved faster than he expected and soon they were standing at the loading gate. After a short wait, his mother managed to decipher a loud speaker message to mean that his flight would now start loading. People began to shuffle forward and suddenly there was only time for a quick hug from his mother, followed by an encouraging clap on the shoulder from his father, and he was boarding his first plane.

The interior proved to be much roomier and luxuriously furnished than he had expected and he was delighted to find that he had been allocated a window seat. Settling into it, he was able to watch the final preparations for departures outside and also to note that it was now beginning to rain.

Soon he heard a door slam and then the engines roared into life, one by one. They quickly settled down to a steady throb, and the sleek aircraft began to move slowly away from the loading area.

A few minutes later they were cleared for take-off and the note of the engines deepened as the plane gathered speed.

Watching the landscape change to a blur, Harry grasped the arms of his seat, not quite knowing what to expect. His attention was diverted by the rain beginning to crawl across the windows, and then they entered the cloud layer which was like a thick fog.

Watching the fog rolling and curling around the aircraft as though it were reluctant to let it through, Harry was dismayed. *We get enough fog at home,* he thought. *How awful if the whole trip is like this.*

Suddenly, the still climbing plane broke through the clouds and the boy gasped at the changed view outside. The gray fog had disappeared as though by magic to be replaced by brilliant sunshine over a fairyland of fleecy white clouds stretching away in all directions with no discernable limits or horizons. He was still staring in fascination when a voice close by asked: "I guess this is your first trip, son?"

Startled he turned to see the man in the next seat regarding him with a smile. "How did you guess?" he asked in surprise.

The other laughed gently, "I could almost hear the '*Ooh's*' and '*Aah's*' when we broke through that cloud cover! Believe me, you will never forget that experience. The same thing happened to me on my first flight nearly fifty years ago, and I can still see it. Actually, anyone who takes off for the first time on a rainy day is lucky, because that kind of thing is likely to happen. On a fine day, it can't."

Harry studied the man as he listened. He saw a stocky individual with white hair, which seemed to accentuate the deep tan of his face. Twinkling blue eyes gave him a general air of good humor. *A nice old guy,* Harry decided. Although he wasn't sure he wanted to talk, he had been brought up to be polite, so he asked the man if he had flown much himself.

"A fair amount. I am a retired airline mechanic. Frank Shaw by name." There was a short pause before he continued, half to himself. "But flying is all pretty routine by now, like riding railroads. When I started, we had to pioneer the routes."

The boy was interested in spite of himself. "Pioneer air routes? Why would anyone want to do that?"

The man looked at him and chuckled. "Well how do you think they all got started? First, they had to be surveyed and runways prepared. Then staff had to be recruited to maintain the planes, if and when they got through. Did you know that the first coast to coast flight in this country took several weeks?"

Harry was amazed. "How could it take so long?"

"Easy! Unreliable planes and engines, no weather service, and practically no navigational aids. That meant no night flying of course." The boy was quiet for a moment as he tried to imagine the country without airlines.

"Even so, they were a lot better off in this country than we were," continued his companion. "When they had to make unscheduled landings, they had no language barrier, and could probably find a hotel nearby. When we landed in some places, we didn't even know if the local tribe would want to attack the plane or worship it!"

Harry was listening wide-eyed. "Where was that?"

"Oh, Africa and the Middle East mostly, although we did get to other areas occasionally."

"Africa and the Middle East?" repeated his listener. "We studied those places in school recently and I thought they were so interesting. I sure would like to go there someday."

"Just make your mind up to do it and one day you will," said Frank. Of course, you won't find things as we did, but it will still be interesting, I promise you."

"How do you mean? I thought things didn't change much out there? I mean the Pyramids and whatnot."

"They haven't changed, but we sure changed other things with the first airplanes! You see, it would start out with our Operations people deciding which route they would like surveyed. All the governments concerned had to be contacted for permission to land and make the surveys. Even when we had that permission, we set off for some almost unknown territories, simply hoping for the best."

Harry was now all attention. "You mean yours was the first plane the people had ever seen?"

"Exactly! And, as many of the tribes still believed in witchcraft, you would never believe some of the receptions we got. Sometimes everybody ran away, and occasionally others would want to capture the strange bird!

"Of course, we had a language barrier almost everywhere. None of them spoke English and some of their languages we had never even heard of. We always managed to get through to them somehow, though. One particular case I recall we had great difficulty. The village chief was so used to accepting gifts from visitors that he assumed our plane was a gift from his God behind the moon. The only problem he could see was how we were going to get back to where we had come from. He was really sorry he could offer us only donkeys and camels!"

His listener was following every word. "What kind of planes were you using?"

"Lumbering landplanes, with no air conditioning, and a top speed of not much more than 100 miles an hour! When we ran into a headwind, we could barely keep up with the few motor vehicles on the ground, or even some of the wild animals!"

"You saw herds of wild animals? Big herds?"

"You bet! They were our big tourist attraction and we used to fly very low over them to raise the spirits of our passengers. It gave them a real thrill and they just loved it! Those deer, giraffes, and even rhino, used to show quite a turn of speed. It wasn't usually for long though, because they would reach the nearest trees and disappear quickly."

The rattle of the trolley in the aisle attracted their attention and soon a smartly uniformed stewardess was serving them a tasty lunch. So tasty, in fact, that all conversation stopped.

Glancing out of the window, Harry saw that they were flying very high and the Earth was little more than a blur with wisps of clouds drifting across it. Nothing much of interest there, so he turned to his companion again. To his dismay, Frank appeared to be about to settle down for a little nap.

*Just as he was getting interesting,* thought the boy. *I wonder how I can get him to carry on?*

"Were you ever on the ground near the wild animals?" he asked boldly. To his great relief, Frank came back to life and didn't seem to mind the question.

"Oh, occasionally, because some of the time we were really out in the bush using tents or thatched huts, or whatever was available. Even when we got the route going, accommodation could be a problem. The planes of those days rarely carried more than twenty people and they flew only in daylight. There were no night landing facilities until much later, which meant that passengers and crew could go to bed every night. That was fine at night stops such as Cairo where there was plenty of local accommodation and entertainment available, but not so good in the African bush where we had to be on guard for animals searching for food."

"Did you shoot many animals?"

Frank shook his head. "No, I'm not a hunter. I had enough trouble keeping small things out of my quarters – snakes, scorpions, tarantulas, and whatnot."

"Nothing bigger?" Harry sounded a little disappointed and his companion had to chuckle.

"Oh, we came close enough occasionally. Mechanics had to service the aircraft engines at each night stop and I recall one night stop in Central Africa when things got a little scary. There were three of us, and one found that his job was going to take an hour longer than expected, so he asked my buddy and I to leave him and make sure supper was kept hot. We left him one of the two small trucks to drive himself back in and return to base, about a mile away.

"Three hours later he hadn't returned and we figured something must be wrong, so we drove back to the airfield. It was a brilliant moonlit night and the aircraft was plain to see. We had left the other mechanic on a high, spindly platform in front of the engines and we could just make out that he was still there, apparently sitting doing nothing. As we drove up, he shouted 'Watch out! Lion!'

"We couldn't see anything at first except he was pointing downward. Then, by looking again carefully, we were able to make out the form of a full-grown lion sitting at the base of the platform. Waiting hopefully, I suppose.

"We had no weapons with us and at first, we were not sure what to do. Then I had an idea. Locking both doors, I drove towards the animal, slipping the clutch steadily and making the engine roar unevenly. I hoped the racket would scare the lion away, but he just sat there until we were almost on top of him. Then he took off, right over our hood, and disappeared into the bush! We were all shook up and the man on the platform must have set some sort of a record scrambling down and into the truck!

"Next morning, we took a rifle with us, just in case. We didn't see our visitor again though, and we made sure none of the passengers heard anything about it."

The boy was listening with rapt attention. "Gee! I wish I could have adventures like that! Did you ever see the Pyramids and the River Nile?"

The man paused and seemed to be looking way back throughout the years.

"Well, I was based in Egypt for some time and I was able to see the Pyramids clearly from my quarters. They were a few miles away, but I remember how close they seemed every morning in the clear air before the heat haze set in. I visited them a few times and even climbed the biggest one. As for the Nile, we ran our main route as close to it as possible, so we saw plenty of it, crocodiles, hippos, and all."

Harry was trying to visualize living in such places. "What about the desert?" he asked, anxious to keep the man going. "Did you spend any time there?"

"Desert!" the word seemed to amuse the storyteller. "Did you know that if you were to take Cairo as the center, you could go almost a thousand miles in any direction except north and find nothing but sand? To the north there is the Mediterranean Sea, of course. In fact, there is so much featureless desert out there that when we flew east from Cairo, we followed oil company pipelines as much as possible. They were laid on top of the sand and sure simplified navigation!

"We had to set up bases in the desert sometimes and we really learned about sand and what it can do. Those vast open spaces are subject to sandstorms known by such names as Sirocco, Haboob, Khamsin, etc. according to particular areas. They are all awesome. First, a sand-colored cloud appears on the horizon. It approaches slowly, growing larger all the time until it towers a thousand feet or more in height and as much as a mile across. It advances silently and ominously, until the cloud is almost overhead, then everything goes absolutely still and quiet. Not even a dog barks.

"Soon, the storm explodes with hot, hurricane-force winds loaded with sand. Visibility drops to zero while the sand blasts everything with enough force to strip paint from buildings and vehicles. You wonder if it is going to take your skin off too while it gets into your eyes, ears, and mouth as well as inside your clothing. The sand feels like pure grit when it strikes, and yet it leaves behind a film as fine as flour dust. I expect I swallowed enough sand to fill a child's playbox." Frank stopped and regarded his engrossed listener with a sly smile, then added, "And that is why camels have such beautiful long eyelashes!"

This brought such a startled expression to the boy's face that he had to laugh out loud. "They do you know. They need them to shield their eyes from the glare of the sun as well as protection from blowing sand."

Harry was just about to ask another question when his companion said, "I don't think I have talked so much in years. I guess I don't often get such a willing listener. But what about you? Where are you headed and why?"

Pleased that such a man could be so interested, the boy was soon telling him all about his opportunity to sail on a schooner after spending all of his life on a farm. Frank listened closely and became almost as enthusiastic as he was!

"This really is a special time for you. Your first aeroplane flight, followed by your first sea voyage. That sounds like adventuring to me!"

Harry felt a glow inside, to be told that by a man who had spent so much of his life adventuring around the world was something special. His thoughts were interrupted by a voice on the intercom announcing that they would land in Portland in fifteen minutes.

The boy looked at his watch in disbelief. "I can't believe the time has gone so quickly!" he said.

"Neither can I," agreed his companion. "Although it usually does when you have an interesting partner."

A few minutes later they were shaking hands. "Thank you for making my first trip so interesting," said Harry. "I sure hope we meet again."

"Possible," smiled Frank. "I still get around a lot. Good luck."

# Chapter Two

## *A SHOCK AT DAWN.*

Despite his fears, Harry had no difficulty in recognizing his Uncle Fred. After all, he had seen photographs of this tall, smiling man often enough. And the youth with him was presumably cousin Peter.

"Hello Harry!" the man greeted him. "I guessed it was you. This is Peter."

The two boys shook hands and murmured greetings. Harry noticed that the other was slightly taller but not so heavily built as himself. Peter had a strong grip, but what struck Harry most was the humorous glint in his gray eyes which gave him the impression that the owner found the world an amusing place in which to live.

"Come on," urged Mr. Fred Pallant. Let's get your bags in the car and we'll have you home in half an hour. Supper should be about ready when we arrive."

During the drive through the outskirts of Portland, Harry was kept busy answering questions about his parents, about the farm, and how he enjoyed his first flight. His uncle chuckled at his impression of the flight. "The first flight is likely to stick in your memory," he said. "Mine was in a small trainer and I still remember it vividly because the pilot did a few stunts and then, after we landed, asked me if I had enjoyed it. I was absolutely speechless but he took my silence for enthusiasm. So he took off again and repeated the whole performance! I could hardly walk when we landed again!"

Presently the car swung into a long driveway leading to a tall, Victorian style house almost hidden by trees. The large front garden was a profusion of flowers and Harry could not help thinking how his mother would love such a display.

"This is the place," announced Peter as the car stopped. "Let me take one of your bags, Harry." He led the way into a large hall dominated by a broad oak staircase with gleaming banisters. Rooms opened on either side and the visitor could see that the house was furnished more for comfort than style. Somehow it seemed to have an air of relaxation.

The noise of their arrival brought a woman and two girls from the kitchen. *This must be Aunt Ivy,* thought Harry as the woman approached. She was fairly tall, with a trim figure and an infectious smile. She greeted him with a hug and a kiss. "It's nice to have you, Harry. What a pity your parents couldn't come too. These are your cousins – Wendy and Pauline."

The two pretty girls, as tall as their brother, advanced smilingly and Harry was suddenly afraid that they too were going to kiss him! He was relieved when they merely shook hands and identified themselves. They impressed him as quiet, gentle girls probably more likely to be seen than heard.

"Come into the kitchen," said his aunt. "Supper is almost ready and you can tell us all about your journey while we finish it."

There was room for everybody in the big, old-fashioned kitchen, but no sooner had they sat down when the room shook as something thudded heavily against the back door.

"Let him in, somebody," said Mr. Pallant. "Or we'll need a new door."

Wendy moved quickly and swung the door wide open. A black object shot into the kitchen and immediately stiffened four legs in a desperate attempt to stop its slide before colliding with the opposite wall. It was an American Cocker Spaniel, and he managed to skid to a stop only just in time.

"This is Pip," announced Wendy and at the sound of her voice, the dog leapt up high enough to lick her face, almost knocking her over. Sensing a stranger in the room, he began sniffing cautiously around Harry's shoes. The farm aroma apparently entranced him, because after savoring it thoroughly, he stretched himself across them and promptly went to sleep.

"Good old Pip!" said Peter. "Full speed and stop are the only two things he knows."

"Supper is ready," announced Mrs. Pallant. "Everybody into the dining room."

It proved to be an enjoyable meal, and Harry began to feel relaxed. There had been some small doubts at the back of his mind about being able to fit in with a strange family, especially one with several children. At home, meals were quiet, but here there was almost constant chatter and frequent laughter.

Harry's uncle had a dry sense of humor and he soon had the guest feeling like a member of the family. The girls surprised him by being full of fun, as often as not at the expense of their brother, although Peter took it all in good spirits.

"It really is nice having you, Harry," said his aunt. We weren't sure if your parents would be able to manage without you."

"They insisted that I come. I know they would have loved to have come too, especially Dad."

"No doubt about that," said Mr. Pallant. "Old Vic would really enjoy sailing with us. But he did as he said he would—he put the oar over his shoulder and he stepped out."

There was a momentary silence at the table. "I don't remember seeing any oars on the farm," said Harry, a little puzzled.

"Just a moment," put in Mrs. Pallant. "How did oars get into this conversation?"

Her husband laughed as he looked around at the baffled group. "Perhaps I should explain! There is an old saying among sailors which you hear whenever things get rough—prolonged bad weather or an uncomfortable ship, for example. Then you are bound to hear someone say, 'When I get ashore after this trip, I am going to put an oar over my shoulder and walk inland with it until somebody asks me what that thing on my shoulder is for. Only then I will know I am as far from the sea as I can get, so I'll buy a farm and settle down! Well, Vic didn't actually carry an oar to Missouri, but he did accomplish the rest. His home is where his heart is now, and good luck to him."

"I suppose that is what you call a sea yarn," sniffed Mrs. Pallant amid chuckles from the others.

"Anyhow, Harry," continued her husband. "If this weather holds, I think we can promise you a really interesting vacation—an unusual one anyway! Tomorrow, we have a few finishing-off jobs to do on the *Seawolf* before we take her out on a trial run. Then, if all goes well, we should be able to sail in a couple of days."

Harry felt a glow at the very idea. "The *Seawolf* must be the schooner," he said. "How big is it?"

"It's a fifty-footer," offered Peter. "And I chose the name!"

"It's an old ship," continued his father. "I managed to pick it up at a very reasonable price because it had been the subject of an insurance claim. We spent the whole winter refitting her and we are all looking forward to enjoying the results of our labors."

"I'll say," said Peter. "I worked like a dog all winter."

"That's true," agreed Pauline. "You and Pip did about the same—watching and getting in the way!"

While Peter struggled to think of a suitable retort, Harry was able to put in a few words. "I know I'm going to enjoy it. I've often read about adventures on schooners and wished such adventures could happen to me. I still won't believe it until we actually do sail!"

When the meal was over, Peter suggested a walk along the beach. The girls eagerly assented, and Harry needed no more encouragement than Pip did. The beach was only a few blocks away and soon they were walking along on soft sand enjoying a cool, salt-laden breeze. Lazy breakers were pounding the sloping shore and Pip galloped happily up and down, just out of reach.

To Harry's unaccustomed eyes, the sea seemed to be dotted with lights in all directions and he soon had Peter explaining the differences of between the lights of the fishing boats, navigation aids, and ships. As he listened, he drew a deep breath of satisfaction. "At last! I've always wanted to see the ocean because I've heard so much about it from my father. Did you know that he and your father were sailors together when they were young?"

"We ought to," chuckled Wendy. "We've heard about it often enough!"

"I'll wager they were a rollicking pair in those days!" mused Peter.

"Imagine living away from the sea," remarked Pauline. "With no swimming, sailing, or beachcombing, I don't think I could stand it!"

"What do people do on a farm, anyway?" asked her brother.

"There's always plenty to do," Harry assured him.

"Like work, I suppose," put in Wendy. "Pete meant what else?"

"How do you know what I meant?" he demanded. "I'm quite capable of explaining what I meant, without any help from you."

"You are?" cried Wendy, in mock surprise. Then she leapt nimbly to one side as Pete charged towards her. The sudden movement attracted Pip's attention and he leapt up to meet his master. Unfortunately, at that moment, Peter was off balance, and a moment later he was flat on his back with the dog gleefully licking his face. Without a moment's hesitation, his sisters sat on him, and Harry had to giggle at their ability to act as one without prior discussion.

"Let that be a lesson to you!" observed Pauline. "Never attack poor, defenseless girls!"

"Defenseless my foot!" roared Pete. "You should show more respect for your elder brother."

"Older!" chortled Pauline. "Listen to him, Harry, he is just thirty-five minutes older than I am, and only fifteen minutes older than Wendy."

"Of course. I keep forgetting that you are triplets," said Harry. "That must be something really special. I never had a brother or sister."

"Well, it was something of an occasion, according to Mother," said Wendy. "Our picture was on the front page of several newspapers, and there was quite a fuss about it at the time. Even the doctors at the hospital had never seen triplets before. They are much more common now, though."

With two heavy girls and a dog pinning him down, Pete was helpless and had to admit defeat so he was allowed to get back up. "I think we should go back now," he remarked as he brushed himself clear of sand. "We've walked a fair distance."

They retraced their steps chattering gaily and were soon back at the house. As they entered, Harry found himself yawning.

"I guess you've had a pretty full day, Harry," observed his uncle. "You can go up to bed whenever you'd like. We won't be long."

"I hope you don't mind sharing with Pete," put in his aunt. "The two girls share a room and we have no spare."

"Of course I don't mind," Harry assured her. "In fact, I've often wished I had a room-mate."

"Did you hear what the boy said?" asked Wendy in an awed tone to nobody in particular. "It's my big ambition to have a room of my very own as soon as possible."

"Me too," declared her sister.

"Oh, you girls would soon miss each other," said their mother. "At least you have more room now than when Anita shared with you too. Although you managed then pretty well."

"Anita is our elder sister," Pauline explained to Harry. "She is a commercial artist and left home a few months ago to take a job in Halifax, Nova Scotia. We miss her, although we are glad of the extra space."

"She left just before we bought the schooner," said Mr. Pallant. "So, we plan to sail up the coast and visit her on the way so she can see it, and hopefully spend some time with us."

"How about something to eat?" asked Wendy suddenly. "It seems like hours since we've had supper."

"It is— nearly two!" observed her mother drily. "Get what you want quickly and then off to bed. We have a busy day tomorrow."

Half an hour later as they all said goodnight, the girls reminded Pete to give them a call next morning as usual. Harry was soon climbing into bed, thoroughly tired but very happy. He was thrilled to find that his new friends shared his own fun-loving outlook on life. He felt sure this was going to be the best vacation he ever had.

"It must be great having a couple of sisters," he mused aloud.

Pete was still undressing and paused to stare at his new room-mate. "What did you say?" he asked, as though unable to believe his ears.

"I am the only one," murmured Harry sleepily.

"Oh well, I suppose sisters are better than nothing," chuckled Pete. "Although, I often wish I had a brother to help me keep my end up!"

"Believe me—" began Harry, only to fall asleep in mid-sentence. His cousin looked at him in surprise and then, putting out the light, continued his preparations in the dark.

Harry slept soundly and awoke at his usual time. Quickly realizing where he was, he leapt out of bed and called to his cousin, "Come on, Pete! It's morning. How about a swim or a walk along the beach?"

The other boy grunted. Opening one eye a mere slit, he asked mechanically, "What time is it?"

"Five o'clock!"

Pete opened his eyes momentarily and sucked in his breath. He appeared to be having some difficulty in collecting his wits.

Eventually, he managed a strangled, "Did you say *five o'clock?*"

"That's right," replied Harry cheerfully. "And it looks as though it is going to be another fine day."

"It probably will – later," sighed Peter. Then, after a short pause he added, "Anyhow, you shower first, and on your way give the girls a call in."

"Sure thing," replied Harry as he pulled on his dressing gown. Soon he was tapping on the door of the next room. There was no reply so he tapped a little louder and longer.

Finally, a sleepy voice asked, "Who's there?"

"It's Harry. I just wanted to let you know the time."

A few moments later the door opened and a tousled, sleepy-eyed Pauline peered at him in the half light.

"What did you say?"

"I said I wanted to let you know the time," announced Harry brightly.

"What's going on?" demanded Wendy faintly from her bed.

"It's Harry come to tell us it's five o'clock," reported Pauline. "The poor boy. Even in a strange bed he should have been asleep before this."

"But I have been asleep," protested the boy. "I slept all night and I'm up now because it's morning."

Pauline gaped at him in speechless wonder and during her silence, her sister came to life.

"Some kind of nut," declared Wendy. "Open the door wider."

Mechanically Pauline obeyed, assuming her sister wanted to be able to talk to Harry direct. But Wendy had other ideas. A pillow whizzed past Pauline's ear and slammed Harry full in the face. It also caught him off balance and he sat down with a thud which shook the house. Whereupon there came a seaman like roar from the master bedroom. "What's going on there?"

Pauline quickly closed the door and jumped back into bed with a giggle – which died the moment she learned that it was her pillow that had been used as a missile.

Harry hurried back to ask Pete what was wrong with the girls, but his cousin was fast asleep, with a smile on his face.

*Bertram Smith*

## Chapter Three

# THE *SEAWOLF*
# AND THE FLYING DOG.

Unable to think of anything else better to do, Harry got back into bed wondering how many hours he would have to lie awake before these city people would begin their day. Moments later, it seemed he was being shaken by a fully dressed Pete. "Come on sleepwalker! It's past eight o'clock and breakfast is almost ready."

At breakfast the early morning incident was discussed and analysed with considerable amusement by the family. "If you want to turn this gang out at five a.m., you'll have to use dynamite!" chuckled Mr. Pallant.

"But we always get up at five on the farm," protested Harry. "Except on Sundays, when we lie in until six."

"Lie in until six!" shrieked Pauline. "I'm surprised the cows and chickens don't complain!"

Harry was happy to join in the general laughter, relieved that no one was upset. At the end of the meal his uncle announced that they would all leave for the boatyard as soon as everyone was ready.

"How far is it?" asked Harry curiously.

"Less than half a mile," said his aunt. "We could easily walk but I'm afraid riding has become a habit."

"What about Pip?" asked Wendy anxiously. "Can he come?"

Her father hesitated a moment and then shook his head. "I know he would like to, but this is an important day for us and we are going to have to concentrate on what we are doing. He has never been to sea before and I am afraid he might get in the way. Also, while we are learning to handle a strange boat he could fall, or get knocked overboard. After all, the decks are very narrow."

Pete and his sisters looked disappointed, but Wendy felt it the most. "He won't be happy without us," she murmured, stroking Pip's head as he sat listening.

"I know that," admitted Mr. Pallant. "But I'm afraid that in this case he wouldn't be happy with us either." To change the subject, and lighten the gloom, he went on. "If this trial run goes all right today, we'll go for a shakedown cruise tomorrow and make a full day of it. Then you will all have a chance to get used to handling the boat."

"Shakedown cruise?" the term was unfamiliar to Harry.

"That's a naval term, Harry. When a warship is first commissioned it is usually taken for a short cruise to allow the crew to get used to the ship and also each other."

"I'm afraid it will take me a long time to get used to a boat," said the boy doubtfully.

"Don't worry," replied his uncle reassuringly. "We are all out of practice and for that reason I have asked an old sailor friend of ours to come along today to help us get the feel of our new boat."

The triplets were immediately all attention. "Not Old Spiff?" asked Pete eagerly.

"Of course!"

"Fine! I love to listen to that old man spinning sea yarns." Pete turned to his cousin. "He has been all over the world in sailing ships and he can spin yarns by the hour. He is well known around here, but nobody ever calls him anything but Spiff."

"I hope he's forgotten the last time he saw us," said Pauline.

"So do I," chuckled Wendy. "He hasn't seen us since the time we fixed his bell!"

Peter laughed at the memory and explained: "Old Spiff lives on his own boat and when he is onboard always rings the bell to show the time – from one to eight bells. I guess it reminds him of the old days. Well, one day we glued some sponge rubber inside the bell, and then hid to watch him try to ring eight bells. When he did his face was really worth watching!"

"What strange names you have for people around here," remarked Harry. "How could anybody possible have a name like 'Spiff'?"

"I've often wondered," said Pete.

"So far as I understand it," put in his father, "Spiff is short for Spiffy, which used to indicate a fancy dresser in the days when he was a young man. Apparently, he was noted for his fancy vests, pants, and socks. He still likes to display his collection of vests and I don't think I've ever seen him wear the same one two days in a row. I try to remember to compliment him on whichever one he happens to be wearing, although sometimes I forget. Now let's get moving."

A few minutes later, Wendy gloomily locked the door on a downcast dog and joined the others in the car. Soon they arrived at Stinson's Boatyard, a busy place with boats of all types both afloat and on ashore. As their car pulled into the parking space, a ruddy-faced little man strolled up wearing a peaked cap and blue reefer jacket, opened to reveal a polka dot vest.

"Hello Spiff," greeted Mr. Pallant. "That's a sharp looking vest you are wearing today. I never seem to see you wearing the same one twice. How many do you have?"

The old man, obviously pleased, swung his jacket open wider to show off the vest. "Glad you like it! I've no idea how many I own. Dozens at least. They used to make the ladies notice me – but not anymore!" Then as he noticed Mrs. Pallant, he swept off his cap and revealed his shiny bald head, which could easily have been confused with shiny mahogany. A thin fringe of jet-black hair seemed to accentuate the gloss. "Good morning, Ma'am. I see you've brought the gang with you."

"Yes," she smiled. They are all here, plus a visitor. I hope they won't be any trouble to you."

"That's all right," he assured her with a broad wink at the four. "Even these rapscallions shouldn't be able to get into mischief on a boat out to sea. Although maybe I had better stow the bell away!"

Gathering up their gear, they followed the old man towards the pier at the end of the boatyard. "There she is," announced

Pete. Harry gasped with admiration. He had not expected anything like this sleek boat resplendent in fresh black paint and gleaming varnish. The name *"SEA WOLF"* stood out boldly in gold lettering across the stern.

"Is that her?" Harry asked in awe. "I imagined a much smaller boat. Just look at the height of those masts!"

"Wait until you go aloft," grinned Pete. "It's a real thrill."

"And wait until you see her under a full spread canvas," put in old Spiff. "I guarantee she'll be a sight to make your eyes sparkle."

As soon as they were all aboard, Harry wanted to explore the vessel, so Pete showed him around and explained the layout. The interior proved to be roomier than might be expected. Two cabins paneled in mahogany stretched across the full width of the boat and they were connected by a narrow companion way. This in turn opened into a tiny, but well equipped, galley on one side, and a neat little washroom on the other. The two spacious cabins had wide settees along each side and a table in the middle, all of which could easily be converted into beds so that each cabin could sleep three people comfortably.

The forward cabin was intended for Mrs. Pallant and the girls. The after one, being nearer the controls, was for her husband and the boys. The controls were next to the steering wheel on the bulkhead just outside the cabin door in a small open cockpit near the stern.

When the boys regained the deck, they found the two men looking aloft. "The job has to be done," said Spiff. "So, we may as well do it before we go."

"What has to be done, Dad?" asked Pete.

"The old signal halyards had rotted away, and I have the new line for the job, but we just never got around to it." He had a new coil of thin rope in his hand and Harry wondered where on earth it could go. The rigging looked a maze to him already, although he would've hesitated to say so.

"Where do the signal halyards go?" Pete wanted to know.

The old man was quick to explain. "You see those flat shapes at the very top of each mast?" he pointed and the boys were able to identify the objects. "Well, they are the trucks and in each one there is a small pulley block to take these halyards. They have to be rove through from underneath and then down from the top before being brought back to the deck."

"I think I had better do the job myself," said Mr. Pallant.

"Oh no you won't!" injected his wife who had just emerged on deck with the girls. "There are no steps at the top anyhow."

"Those rope steps are called ratlines, Mom," said Pete. "I'm sure I could go up there. How about you, Harry?"

Harry had been studying the situation. The masts seemed to become taller the more he studied them, and that top corner without any steps could be difficult. "Well—" he began.

"All you have to do is shin up a pole," said the old man impatiently. "Let me show you."

"Oh no you don't!" said Mr. Pallant quickly. "Not at your age! How are you on heights, Harry?"

"I never have any trouble when I work on our barn roof, and that is pretty high."

"Let the boys do it," suggested Spiff. "I did all the jobs like that before I was their age. Although I did have a rope's end to encourage me," he added with a chuckle.

"We'll do it," said Wendy. "Won't we Pauly?"

Pauline screwed up her eyes as she peered aloft. "Will we?" She seemed very doubtful.

"All right, you boys can do it," announced Mr. Pallant. "Here you are. Tie the line around your waists like this, so it can easily be released. Hold on tightly with one hand when you get to the top, and pass the end of the line up, through the pulley and then over and down again. Be sure to take a couple of turns around your wrist before you come down."

"And do be careful," added his wife.

The two boys leapt into the rigging with a will. Harry found the sagging ratlines strange to climb on, but he could see from the corner of his eye that Pete had obviously done it before, because he was a climbing monkey. By the time Harry was half way up the rigging, his cousin had reached the foot of the topmast and was wrapping his arms around it.

Puffing a little, Harry reached the top of the rigging and paused to peer upward. The topmast, which appear quite short when seen from the deck, now seemed to tower into the sky. *How could it be so tall?* he wondered as he wrapped his arms around it and cautiously edged upwards. Turning his head a little, he could see that Pete was already at the top and hanging on with one hand while he used his other to fumble with the rope around his waist.

Slowly and very carefully, Harry inched his way upward. Surprisingly, it was not proving to be so difficult after all, especially if he did not look down. He had done so once and the deck had seemed very far below, and the others, with their upturned faces, almost tiny.

The wooden truck had come within his grasp almost unexpectedly. Tightening the grip of his legs around the mast, he carefully loosened the rope tied around his waist. He had no difficulty in threading the rope upward through the small pulley, but when he wanted to let go of it in order to grasp it from above, it quickly began to run back again and he almost lost it. He paused to think. What a disgrace it would be if he let the rope fall to the deck.

Pete, who had already finished and was on his way down, would have to do this mast too. Then his brain clicked. Pushing the rope through from underneath until the end hung down in front of his face, he then grasped it with his teeth. Now he could change his grip to thread the rope down through the pulley and then around his wrist. At last!

Pausing to catch his breath, he took the opportunity to admire the unusual view of a busy boatyard from high up. Then he began to slide down very carefully without looking down. It proved to be easier than expected and he thoughtlessly allowed himself to increase speed. He soon realized that the mast was way too slippery for him to grip hard enough with his legs to slow the descent. His heart seemed to crowd in his throat and he had visions of crashing onto the deck below to lie broken and bleeding at the feet of his horror-stricken relatives. Such things did happen, he knew. Then he felt a jolt as his feet hit the top of the steel band holding the rigging, stopping him dead.

Catching his breath, he carried on down the ratlines as though he had planned to come down like that. Reaching the deck, he was congratulated by everybody, but the remarks of Spiff meant the most to him. "Couldn't have done it better myself, young feller. You were a bit slow going up, but you came down like a professional!"

"I didn't do as well as Pete," said Harry. "He went up in half the time."

"I've done it several times before," said Pete. "At least to the top of the rigging, so I had the advantage of you."

"Don't worry," put in his father. "In a couple of weeks you will think nothing of such things. You will all be able to carry out any order swiftly and without hesitation."

"Oh no!" said Pauline.

"I knew there was going to be a catch," said Wendy.

"I suppose I'll be doing all of the cooking," observed their mother.

"Oh, no, my dear," said her husband firmly. "You are the first mate and you must be ready to take over from me in an emergency. On a boat this size, everybody should take a turn at the cooking."

"Quite right," Old Spiff nodded approvingly. While the four youngsters exchanged startled glances.

"Is that alright with you, Harry?" asked his uncle.

"Er— yes, Sir," replied the startled boy.

Mr. Pallant paused. "Well, now. I think we had better cut out the *Sirs* and *Misters.* This is going to be a free and easy vacation, so I think I prefer to be called 'Skipper'. Now, let's get underway. You cast off forward, Spiff, and I'll take care of the stern lines, while these others learn by watching a couple of real professionals at work! I'm going to take her out on the motor until we reach open water. Then we'll see how she behaves under canvas."

"Ay-aye, Skipper!" The old man made his way smartly forward and the mooring lines were quickly cast off. The *Seawolf* began to move slowly ahead and Pauline cried out, "Away we go – at last!"

"Listen!" exclaimed Wendy suddenly. Surprise made everyone quiet for a moment and they heard a short, familiar bark in the distance. "It's Pip!" she yelled excitedly. "Look!"

Sure enough, there was Pip hurtling towards them as though trying to race time itself. He was about fifty yards away and seemed to know exactly where he was headed.

With an exclamation, the skipper put the motor out of gear, while the others kept their eyes on the galloping dog. People in the boatyard stared as he swept by, mouth open and red tongue showing while his ears extended like wings, borne on the wind he was creating.

"Just look at that dog," exclaimed Spiff admiringly. "With his ears like that, you'd swear he is about to take off and fly!"

The gap between the boat and the pier was now about fifteen feet, but it quickly became apparent that the dog did not realise there was any gap.

"Stop, Pip!" screamed Wendy. "You'll fall in the water!"

But the sound of his beloved mistress's voice seemed to spur him on and, with what looked exactly like a wide grin on his face, Pip continued at full speed beyond the edge of the pier.

For one startling moment, it seemed as though those ears had enabled him to fly!

"Oh, for a camera now," murmured Mrs. Pallant, torn between admiration and anxiety.

It was obvious that the dog would fall several feet short of the boat, and when he realized it, his expression changed to one of comical surprise.

Then, as he fell over the edge of the dock, he saw the water coming near, his four paws started paddling furiously so that he was already swimming when he struck the water with a huge splash and promptly disappeared.

"Oh, Pip!" cried Wendy in dismay.

A moment later a gleaming black head popped to the surface close alongside.

"There he is!" shouted Pete. "Shall I go after him?"

"No, no!" roared his father. "Pull him out with a boathook. Quickly, before he goes under the boat." Pete grabbed a long-handled boathook from the cabin roof and swung it hurriedly.

CLONK.

"Hey!" howled Pauline. "Go easy. That was my head!"

Pete turned in surprise and the long shaft swung wildly again.

"Hold it!" roared Old Spiff. "Better let me take that before you either brain one of us or harpoon the dog!"

Pip was now trying to climb the smooth side of the boat. Leaning over, the old salt skillfully hooked the dog's collar and with a heave, swung him up and onto the deck.

Pip was too surprised to move for a moment, but after a quick shake which showered everybody within reach, he hurled himself at Wendy, almost knocking her overboard.

"Take that dog forward before he drowns us all," ordered the skipper. Then he added thoughtfully, "It would be interesting to know how Pip got out of a locked house. You did lock it, Wendy?"

"Yes, I did," replied Wendy truthfully.

"Then how could he get out?"

"Maybe a window was left open... or something," Wendy was avoiding her father's eye. A window had indeed been left open a little, but she omitted to mention that she had opened it wider, hoping that Pip would find it.

"Very peculiar," commented her father drily. "Well, he's here now, so we'll have to take him along." He put the motor in gear again and the schooner moved slowly ahead.

Harry was holding on to a stay near the wheel and, expanding his chest, he took a deep breath of the clear air. "Ah!" he murmured with satisfaction.

The skipper laughed at such obvious pleasure. "I knew you would like it! Of course, it isn't always like this. We are lucky to have such fine weather for our first trip."

Harry looked up at the clear dome of the sky and then at the deep blue sea, ruffled by a gentle breeze from the north. How his father would envy him now!

# Chapter Four

## *FIRE!*

The channel out to sea was marked by wooden posts at intervals along each side. These posts made convenient perches for seagulls, and the birds watched solemnly as the boat moved slowly along.

"This must be seagull alley!" said Pete with a grin.

"There is my post," declared Spiff suddenly, as they passed one with no seagull sentinel.

"What do you mean?" asked Harry while the others looked puzzled. Spiff looked at them with a straight face. "Surely you know that old sailors turn into seagulls when they die. That post is being reserved for me when my time comes."

He waved his hand at the row of birds. "Some of these are probably old shipmates of mine. In fact, I'm sure that one was." He pointed to the nearest post. "He was Bos'un with me on the *Pamir* and he looked exactly like that in real life." Everybody stared at the bedraggled, dejected-looking bird and then back to Spiff. His face was still straight, but his eyes gave the game away.

Mr. and Mrs. Pallant smiled when Wendy cried out, "You old fibber. It's not true!"

The old man gave a rumbling chuckle. "Well, just you remember to check that post after I'm gone," he added as the others broke into roars of laughter.

A few minutes later they were clear of the channel and in the open sea. The schooner seemed to lift herself as she entered salt water as though eager to be off.

"Well, she handles fine with the motor," said the skipper. "How about trying her under sail now, Spiff?"

"Aye-aye," responded the seadog smartly. "We'll set that foresail first. Come on you 'lubbers and I'll show you how to set sails."

The four nearly fell over each other in their eagerness to follow him. Swiftly, the old sailor cast off the lashing securing the foresail and the passed the end of the thin line to Harry.

"Here, haul on this handsomely."

"Eh?" The boy was startled. "What does being handsome have to do with it?"

There was a general laughter when Spiff patiently explained that 'handsomely' means, in the language of the sea, slowly and with care. "Now, haul away!"

The foresail was quickly on its way up the forestay and then, in short order, the main and mizzen were set. As Spiff trimmed them to take maximum advantage of the breeze the *Seawolf* heeled over as though pleased to be back in her natural element.

The four gazed upward in awe at what seemed to them to be a huge spread of canvas. "Just look at those sails," breathed Wendy. "I had no idea they would be so big!"

"I expected them to be the size of bedsheets," agreed Pauline.

After a while, Spiff took the wheel and demonstrated how to change course while taking every advantage of the wind. Then, steering on course again, he said to Peter, who happened to be the nearest, "No, Bos'un, you come to try your hand at steering."

"Aye-aye, Sir!" grinned the boy as he scrambled onto the platform behind the wheel. He was surprised to find how little movement was required to alter course. In fact, it was difficult to avoid oversteering, and for a while the *Seawolf* sailed a somewhat zig-zag course.

"Don't grip the wheel," said Spiff. "Hold it lightly and treat it gently."

"Can I have a try?" asked Wendy a few minutes later.

"You are going to, whether you want to or not!" retorted the old salt. "I am going to make helmsman of you all."

An hour later, everybody, including Mrs. Pallant, had taken a turn at the wheel and experienced the thrill of handling a boat under sail. Harry was really delighted. "Wait until Dad hears about this," he chuckled. "He'll be so jealous!"

The skipper was highly pleased with their performance. "You will all make good sailors," he said as he took the wheel again. "Now let me see you all get your lifejackets on in a hurry."

Peter had mentioned that the lifejacket drill was practically a certainty, so no one was surprised. With a wild rush, the four jumped down into the cockpit and made for the cabin doorway. Unfortunately it was very narrow, and they jammed into it like a cork in a bottle.

"I was first!" roared Pete.

"Somebody is on my foot!" howled Harry.

"I didn't realize we were all so fat!" giggled Pauline, as she tried to worm her way through.

"Ladies first!" shouted Wendy from the rear.

"Hurry up, the boat is sinking!" cried her father in mock alarm.

Hearing the commotion, Pip came galloping along the deck and, seeing his playmates apparently enjoying a new game, he took a flying leap into their midst. His weight helped to push the struggling mass through the doorway and the five of them landed in a tangled heap on the cabin floor, with the four barely able to speak for laughing.

At the end of a short session on donning and wearing lifejackets, Mrs. Pallant remarked that everybody must really have been interested not to notice that it was lunchtime. Going below, she returned with a bag containing packets of sandwiches and some cool drinks.

"Good old Mom!" cried Wendy. "I needed this."

It was a glorious, warm day and the four sprawled on the cabin top in the shade of the mainsail to eat in comfort. Meanwhile, Pip had soon found a way out of the cockpit by using the wheel platform as a half-way station, and now he jumped out of the low cabin alongside Wendy to share her sandwiches.

"That dog amazes me," remarked the skipper. "He seems to get around on board just as easily as he does ashore. I thought at least he would take some time to find his sea-legs."

"I expect that having four legs is a great help," said Pete.

"Maybe two of them *are* sea-legs," suggested Pauline with a grin.

As they finished eating, they stretched out comfortably and relaxed. Pete was watching the foam-flecked water swirl along the side of the boat and he heaved a deep sigh. It must have been a sigh of contentment because he said: "This is the life for me! I think when I'm older I'll sail this boat around the world."

"Good idea!" exclaimed Pauline. "We'll come too."

Harry's eyes sparkled. "Oh boy! Imagine a trip around the world on a boat like this."

"Well, why don't you come too?" Pete spoke as though the trip was already arranged and he was leaving the next day.

"Can I?" Harry was quite carried away with the idea.

His aunt smiled at all the enthusiasm. "Before you all leave, would you mind helping to clear away the remains of lunch?"

"I think we had better come about now and set a course for home," announced her husband. "Watch your heads on the boom." He brought the *Seawolf* smartly around on the other tack and everybody ducked to allow the long boom to pass over their heads when the wind caught the sails from the other side.

"Nice work," commented Spiff approvingly.

"How is it you are such an expert on boat sailing, Spiff?" asked the skipper. "I thought you were a big-ship man."

"I was," agreed the old man. "But on nearly every ship, I was given the job of Coxswain of the Captain's Gig. It was supposed to be an honor reserved for the best Coxswain on the ship, but it had plenty of headaches. Going alongside in all weathers could be tricky at times. There were no auxiliary motors then, and oars were used only when it was absolutely unavoidable."

The *Seawolf* heeled over to a freshening breeze as the others grouped themselves around the old salt so that they could hear what he was saying.

"Did you ever sail a boat a long way?" asked Pauline.

Spiff puffed his pipe as though he was looking back in time through the smoke. "I've done some pretty lengthy trips," he said, "But I guess the longest one was in the South China Sea."

"In an open boat?" asked Harry, wide-eyed.

"Yes!" chuckled the seadog. "In an open boat about half the length of the *Seawolf.* Luckily we had fine weather, but the trip lasted a week and we ran out of food on the third day."

"Why did you do it?" asked Pete.

"Not from choice, I assure you. I was on the *Teresa*, a big four masted barque carrying a full cargo of coal, and we had to abandon ship because she caught fire."

Obviously reliving those far off days, he relit his pipe and continued. "I remember I was at the wheel, watching one of those lurid dawns you get in those parts, when I noticed the third mate doing something at one corner of the main hatch. He told us afterwards that he had seen what he thought might be a wisp of smoke curling up from the hold ventilator. Being young and inexperienced, he didn't know any better than to open the hatch to find out.

"He jumped back with a yell when a blast of flaming gas took off his eyebrows and most of his hair. Fortunately, the Bos'un came along just then and clamped the hatch back in place. Then we all realized that we had a fire down below which might have been smoldering for days or even weeks. If it had, we would be lucky if we had a ship much longer.

"During the next twenty-four hours we manned every pump on the ship and poured tons of water into the holds. It was back-breaking hard labor but it didn't seem to do much good. The fire had spread and soon the decks were almost too hot to walk on. By dawn next day, we had pumped so much water into the holds that the ship was barely afloat, but smoke was now pouring from every ventilator and it was obvious that we hadn't much time left.

"The captain gave the order to abandon ship and we cleared those boats away in double quick time. Radio would have been a godsend then, if only there had been such a thing."

"We hove to about a hundred yards away and watched our home for the past year go up in flames. A sight to break your heart. Within a few minutes, pressure building up inside blew the two hatches open and flames shot as high as the mastheads. They ran up the dry sails from the lower main to the skysails, one by one, and then the tarred standing rigging caught. In what seemed like seconds, the whole ship was a flaming mass from stem to stern.

"It wasn't very long before the *Teresa* started to sink as the fire ate through the wooden hull. She went down with great dignity, on an even keel, and the flames and smoke gradually turned into clouds of steam. But not for long. Soon we were able to watch the four topmasts, still burning, seem to hesitate before sinking out of sight."

Old Spiff paused at the memory of those topmasts burning to the end. Then he added: "The following week was a little rough, but we finally made it to Hong Kong, and all was well."

"Gee! What an adventure!" breathed Harry.

"A little rough is probably putting it mildly," commented his uncle. "The boat trip was likely a story in itself."

"Fire at sea is a terrible thing," remarked the old seadog. "And while we are on the subject, I think it might be a good idea to have a fire drill on this ship."

"An excellent idea," exclaimed the skipper. "Will you handle it and continue the training of these young sailors?"

"That I will!" agreed Spiff heartily. "Come on you swabs. There is a fire in the engine compartment. Pass me a fire extinguisher quickly. Jump to it!"

The four jumped in different directions without knowing where to go. "Where are the extinguishers, anyway?" demanded Pete, remembering only that the boatyard had installed them.

"That is something you should know," roared the seadog. "I'm the Engineer, being roasted, and you ask me where the extinguishers are? There is one on each side amidships, a small one in the cockpit and a foam type on the foredeck. Get one each, but don't set them off."

Pete jumped for the nearest one, in the cockpit, and the girls went for those on the side decks, while Harry headed for the big two-gallon cylinder up forward. This particular type was set off by turning it sharply upside down, but the boy did not know that.

Eagerly snatching the heavy extinguisher from its holder, he swung it over his shoulder, intending to trot along the side of the deck with it. He received the shock of his life when a jet of foam struck him in the face. Unable to see properly, he quickly swung the cylinder down and clutched it to his chest, but by now it was going full blast, and the nozzle was pointing aft ship, at all of the other bystanders.

The jet of foam sent Spiff's cap flying and then played steadily on his bald head. For one petrified moment the seven people onboard were transfixed. Then the old man opened his mouth to let out a roar, but the jet wavered down his face and into his mouth, so all he could manage was a choking sputter.

When Harry managed to clear his eyes and see what havoc he had caused, he was paralyzed with horror, so the jet continued to play on the hapless seadog.

"Turn it away!" shouted the skipper, finding his voice at last.

Shocked into action, Harry swung the extinguisher quickly to one side, but he was so excited he turned the wrong way, and one by one, the others came under the spray before he managed to direct it overboard. There was a howl from Pete as the foam caught him in one ear and ran down his neck. His mother and sisters hurriedly clutched their hair as the messy stuff enveloped them. The skipper ducked quickly but did not escape entirely. Only Pip was untouched. He was sitting on the foredeck, behind Harry, watching the fun with his head cocked to one side, as though wondering.

Spiff, who was standing near the after end of the cabin, now looked like a snowman. He was covered from head to foot in the frothy foam and he sounded as though he might also be frothing at the mouth. With some difficulty, he cleared his eyes and glared at Harry, who was already shuddering at the ghastly mess he had made.

Everybody was staring at the old man, expecting him to explode at any moment. Suddenly he let out a roar which nearly made Harry jump backwards into the sea. Then the seadog bent over the top of the cabin, shaking, and making weird noises. This made the skipper so concerned that he thumped the man's back in case he was choking.

"Are you alright, Spiff?" he demanded.

The foam-spattered figure finally straightened up and the choking stopped, although the sputtering continued.

"I believe he's laughing!" gulped Pauline.

"Ho! Ho! Ho!" roared Spiff as he tried to wipe his bald head clear of foam. "Funniest thing I ever saw in fifty years at sea!" he gasped. "I wouldn't have believed it if I hadn't seen it with my own eyes!"

Now everybody onboard roared with laughter, although Harry felt more relieved than amused. All hands quickly turned to clear up the mess, still chuckling at the memory.

When they were all settled down again, Spiff explained how each different type of extinguisher should be used, and also emphasizes that an empty one must <u>never</u>, <u>ever,</u> be returned to its holder before it had been refilled. When he was satisfied that they really understood, he relaxed and started to hum a sea chanty. Then he broke into a rollicking song which all the others soon joined in, picking up the fun tune.

"Gee! We are home already," exclaimed Pete as he saw the channel markers ahead. "That was quick."

"Singing makes the time pass easily," said the old man. "That's why we always used to sing when we were heaving and hauling."

"Stand by to drop the sails," ordered the skipper. "I'll take her in on the motor."

Spiff showed the four how to furl and stow each sail, and by the time they were finished, the boatyard was just ahead. Then he demonstrated how to moor a boat safely so that it would not be damaged by rubbing against the pier.

"That was a wonderful cruise," said Mrs. Pallant, as they all stepped ashore.

"Thanks to Spiff," put in her husband.

"Nobody enjoyed it more than I did," declared the old man. "In fact, I haven't enjoyed myself so much for a long time. I'd say thanks are due to these four seamen."

"It's nice of you to say so," said Harry. "But I'm sorry I spoiled your clothes."

"Don't worry lad, this stuff comes off easily. But even if the clothes were ruined, the experience has been worth it! Well, goodbye folks, I'll see you all another day."

After seeing Spiff on his way, the others piled into the car. "Thank goodness it's nearly suppertime," remarked Wendy. "I'm so hungry I could eat a whale!"

"Knowing you, I can believe that!" grinned her brother.

Harry sat back in the car feeling tired, but happy. For one dreadful moment, when he had seen what he had done to all of the others, he had feared that his vacation might come to a sudden end, with him being sent home in disgrace. It had seemed impossible that everybody would take such an incident as a great joke.

"Thank you all for the wonderful time," he said suddenly. "I must write home about it tonight. I hope I'll see Mr. Spiff again," he added. "He is quite the character."

"Oh, I expect you will," said his uncle. "He spends a lot of time around the boatyard, and I've noticed that he has a knack for showing up whenever anybody needs help."

# Chapter Five

## *OUTNUMBERED!*

Harry soon got used to sleeping later in the mornings and by Saturday, he managed to oversleep. The house seemed strangely quiet when he did awake, so he dressed hurriedly and went downstairs.

There was no one around except his aunt who was humming softly to herself as she washed dishes in the kitchen.

"Good morning, Harry," she said cheerfully. "Did you sleep well?"

"Too well, apparently," he replied. "I don't remember ever sleeping so late. Where are Pete and the girls?"

"It's the sea air, I expect. Some people find it very relaxing at first. The three of them have gone to do their volunteer work. They go downtown once a month to help a very old, crippled lady who lives alone. The girls clean house for her and Pete takes care of the yard. They should be home in a little more than an hour. Perhaps you'd like to stroll along to meet them after you've had your breakfast. I've kept it hot for you. Sit down."

"That sounds like a good idea," said the boy as he dug into his bacon and eggs with a will. Which way do I go?"

"Don't rush your food! When you've finished, turn left at our front gate and follow this street until you come to a library on the corner. Then left again, and that street will take you into an old part of town. Keep going until you see an old movie house. It faces the street on which the old lady lives— I can't remember the name of it, but her number is 106. You will probably see Pete working in her front yard, if you haven't already met them on the way."

It was a bright, sunny day and Harry found himself whistling as he set off at a good pace. He stopped whistling in order to suck in a chestful of sea air. It did feel good!

The big library building soon loomed up ahead and he made a left turn as directed. Almost immediately the neighborhood began to change. Pleasant houses gave way to small stores and gradually these started to deteriorate. There were a few people around as he reached the intersection near the run-down movie house.

Just before he was able to turn the corner, he had to pass a narrow alley, and as he did so, four boys slouched from it immediately in front of him. He was about to change course to avoid a collision when the nearest one, who also happened to be the biggest, stared at him closely and said, "Ah! New boy in town, eh?"

Harry paused in his stride and noticed that the other boys, one tall and thin, and the other two smaller and younger, were closing in around him.

Before he could say anything, the bigger boy went on: "Have you any money? We need some for our welfare fund, don't we fellers?' He leered unpleasantly as he spoke, and the others murmured their assent. Obviously he was the leader, and he was big enough to be able to look down on Harry. He was probably older too, but obviously had no pride in his appearance because his chock of red hair looked as though it hadn't seen a comb in a long time.

"I haven't any money," snapped Harry, turning to pass around the big boy. As he did so the others moved in so close around him that he could hardly move without touching at least one of them—something he had no wish to do.

"Let's offer him a bargain," sneered the tall boy. "He can offer us a donation of $5—each!"

Harry was beginning to feel desperate. Why was it at times like this there was rarely anybody nearby? Even the nearest store was boarded up. If only a police car would drive by!

He did have $5 in his wallet, but he saw no reason why he should give it to a bunch of hoodlums. But, what to do? He could hardly expect to beat them all if they attacked him. Perhaps he should attack first. His heart was beginning to pound, and his breathing quickened as he wondered whether it would be best to try to make a break through and run for it.

As he was still trying to decide, three young people swung around the corner, arguing loudly. It was Pete and his sisters! They stopped at the sight of the hold-up.

"Oh, ho," said Pete. "What goes on here?"

"It looks as though they are threatening Harry," whispered Wendy.

"They had better not," said Pauline. Then loudly to the four boys: "Leave him alone!"

The bigger boy looked over his shoulder. "Girls!" he sneered. "What do you know? Beat it and mind your own business."

"Do something, Pete!" commanded Pauline.

Pete was thinking hard. Four against four might be alright, but not when two were girls against rough boys. Then he had an idea. Slowly, he approached the big boy and spoke to him quietly.

The others saw the nasty expression on the leader's face suddenly replaced by an anxious look. "Come on, fellers," he said loudly. "I just thought of something, follow me." He quickly disappeared into the alley, followed by his mates looking puzzled and surprised.

"Let's get away from here, pronto!" snapped Pete as he stepped off at a brisk pace.

The others kept up with him in silence until they were back on their own street. Then they slowed down and Pete found himself very much the center of attention, with the others all speaking at the same time. What on earth had he said to that bully to make him back off like that, they all wanted to know.

Pete stopped and held up his hand for silence. "I simply told him that he had better take his boys away quickly, before they got hurt."

"How could that work?" demanded Wendy impatiently.

Her brother paused, purposely, until the others were ready to jump all over him. "Well, I needed to make up a story quickly!"

"What could you possibly tell him?" queried Harry in awe.

"I told him that if he was going to tackle you, that he should get some help. Well, that got his attention in a hurry!"

Pete paused for effect while the others waited impatiently. "Then I asked him if he noticed how worried Harry was looking. He was looking very worried, and I explained that because the last time he had been attacked it had been by a grown man almost twice his weight, and that man had to be taken to the hospital with a broken arm and a broken leg. I said you were worried because you didn't want to injure anybody! But being a trained circus acrobat, you didn't know your own strength. I also told him I didn't want my sisters to see broken bodies lying in the gutter. Fortunately, just as I finished telling this yarn, Harry flexed his muscles and clenched his fists as though he was really going to mix it up, and I think that helped the lout to make up his mind to beat it!"

"I did that?" Harry tried to remember. "Anyway, I think that is the brainiest thing I've ever known. Thanks, Pete!"

The two girls surveyed their brother critically. "He doesn't look very brainy," observed Pauline at last.

"I never noticed that he was," said her sister. "Anyhow, you did all right, Pete. You saved us from having to beat up that bunch!"

Pete's face crinkled as he exploded into a loud guffaw. "Ho, ho! Did you hear that," Harry!" he gurgled. "That's what is known as a sisterly compliment! The nearest thing to real appreciation a brother can ever expect!"

"Well, I really appreciate what you did," said Harry sincerely.

"Don't mention it," put in Pauline, assuming part of the credit. "It was the least we could do. After all, you are part of the family."

The other three did not, or could not, realise it, but those last words of Pauline's made Harry's day. So far as he was concerned, to be regarded as part of this particular family was as much as anybody could hope for.

They swung along on their way home and Harry found himself whistling again.

The afternoon was spent beachcombing, and although nothing worthwhile showed up, the four of them, and Pip, had a wonderful time. Harry found it all new and very interesting, but had to confess a little disappointment. "I did think I might find something special, like maybe a bottle with a message in it."

The others laughed at his disappointment. "We had the same idea when we first arrived," said Wendy. "But there seems to be a shortage of such things, except in books, of course."

Later on, after doing justice to a hearty supper. They were all relaxing when Pete asked, "Is the shakedown cruise still on for tomorrow, Dad?"

His father looked surprised. "I'd clean forgotten about it. I know I promised you one, but I was assuming that you would all need much more instruction. But after your performance lately, it hardly seems necessary. You all did such a wonderful job, thanks mainly to old Spiff, that I will be glad to take you on as crew without any more instruction. You need experience, of course, but there's only one way to get that."

Everybody else looked both surprised and pleased, especially Harry. He felt really proud to be accepted as a member of this rollicking crew so quickly.

"The *Seawolf* behaved better than I dared hope," continued the skipper. "So now I think we should plan to leave for Halifax on Monday morning. That would give us all day tomorrow to get ready and load the boat."

"We'll need that at least," said his wife. "All the bedding and clothes have to be transported, as well as food. How much food shall we take?"

"Lots," put in Pauline mischievously.

"Enough for a week should do," replied her father. "Plus, some canned goods for emergencies. Clothes shouldn't be much of a problem. After all, this is going to be a relaxing vacation, I hope, so there won't very much dressing up."

"Good!" Wendy said. "I'm glad we are going to be prepared for emergencies. Do you think we might have one—or two?" She sounded almost hopeful.

"Like Spiff being adrift in an open boat," explained Pauline.

"Definitely not!" replied her father. "Now, Pete. If you will fetch my chart case, we'll lay out the courses to be steered."

When the appropriate charts were spread out on the dining table, the boys leaned over on each side of the skipper as he began to lie off the required courses with the aid of parallel rules. When they were lightly penciled in on the charts, he measured the distances with dividers.

Harry was fascinated. He had never seen these maps of the sea before and he was full of questions. Patiently his uncle explained the meanings of the numerous markings as well as such nautical signposts as lighthouses, buoys, beacons, etc.

"It will be a three-legged course," announced the skipper at last. "First, we go east around the southern tip of Novia Scotia, and then north along the coast until we are nearly opposite Halifax, and then almost due west into port. I figure an approximate total distance of 300 miles."

"How long will it take, Dad," asked Pete.

"Well, it's difficult to estimate an average speed when you are dependent on the wind, if any. I'm hopeful that we'll be able to do it in two or three days, keeping going all night, of course."

"Boy!" exclaimed Harry. "This is going to be a real adventure for me. Imagine sailing on a schooner, day and night!"

His aunt returned with the girls to announce that they had made a good start in preparations for loading the proper necessities for the next day.

"That's fine," said the skipper. "And now to bed everybody."

## Chapter Six

## *OFF TO SEA!*

The four slept soundly and it seemed only moments later they heard Mr. Pallant roaring, "All hands on deck!"

Before they had time to respond, he continued, "Get them out of bed, Pip." Bedroom doors were then thrown open to the accompaniment of excited barking.

As their door flew open, Peter tried to get his head under the sheets, but he was not quite quick enough. Pip came hurtling in, touching the floor only once before bouncing on top of him and frantically licking his face. Then without warning, the dog leapt across to the other bed.

"Ugh!" gasped Harry as all the breath was knocked out of him. "He does that to all of us whenever he gets the chance," chuckled Pete. "You may as well get up now!"

After a quick breakfast, the four started to load the car, closely watched by Pip.

"What about Pip?" whispered Harry. "Is he coming this time?"

Pete and his sisters looked at each other. "It hasn't been mentioned," said Pauline. "I wonder if Mom has asked a neighbor to look after him. She has done sometimes before."

"If we don't ask, we can't be refused," put in Wendy practically. "We'll put him on the floor in the back of the car and keep him quiet until we reach the boat. Dad won't want to turn back then."

"How can we keep him quiet on the floor?" demanded her brother. "You know he always wants to look out the window." "We'll manage somehow," said Wendy. "We are not going to leave him behind. If necessary, we'll put our feet on him!"

"Poor old Pip," chuckled Harry. "He'll wonder what on earth is happening. But when shall we put him in the car? At the last minute?"

"Dad's going to telephone for the weather report just before we leave," declared Pete. "That will be the time."

Half an hour later, all was ready and the skipper announced that the four could be getting in the car while he obtained the weather report, and Mrs. Pallant checked all the doors and windows in the house.

"How the heck are we all going to squeeze in here?" demanded Pete as he surveyed the mass of bags, coats, etc. already piled in the back of the car.

"We'll manage," said Pauline as she wriggled in. "We couldn't get any more into the trunk, so it had to come in here. Let Pip come in now."

The dog was probably surprised when he wasn't allowed to take up his usual position by a window, and even more so when he found himself flat on the floor with several feet resting on his back. But to the relief of all, he accepted the situation calmly.

"He must know he's a stowaway," chuckled Wendy.

A few minutes later, Mr. and Mrs. Pallant got in the car. "The weather report is good," he announced. "So, off to sea we go!"

Pip wagged his tail profusely, hitting the back of the driver's seat. Pete pretended to cough loudly, while the girls began singing a tune from the newest 'Beatles' top radio hit song. Pip continued wagging his tail harder, so Pete nudged Harry for more help.

Harry leapt forward, pretending to accidentally kick the driver's seat, while startling the driver with a fake question of interest, "Uncle, tell me about driving the triplets around town!"

"Why, sure, Harry. Very funny story, one time, the three were quite young, in Kindergarten, and I was driving slowly around a corner. I glanced into the rear mirror, and noticed I've only got two of the triplets. 'Where is Pauline?!' I thundered. Wendy piped in, 'She fell out.' It turned out that the side door had gently opened and Pauline tumbled out of the car, whilst the door closed on the turn, quietly clicking closed once more. No one had said anything, thinking that all grown-ups must know what they are doing, so we must have wanted her to fall out!"

Pip kept wagging his tail. Peter kept coughing. The sisters kept singing.

"What happened next?" Harry queried loudly.

"Well of course we turned back, and there she was on the side of the road, also thinking that we must have wanted her to tumble out! She was completely fine, but what a story eh?"

Everyone shared a laugh at the memory.

Soon the car swung through the gateway of Stinson's Boatyard and the skipper remarked: "You can let Pip up now. He must be very uncomfortable lying down there."

There was a short silence in the car until Wendy had to break it with a giggle. "It always baffles me how grown-ups get to know what's going on, even when they don't see anything."

Her father chuckled, "Maybe it's a good thing they do at times, I expect you will acquire the knack when you have children of your own!" As he was speaking, he stopped the car at the pier near where the *Seawolf* was moored. "Now the quicker all of this stuff is properly stowed onboard, the sooner we can be underway."

The loading was almost completed when old Spiff approached, carefully carrying a fire extinguisher.

"Hello, Spiff," said Mr. Pallant. "Thank you for saving me the job of collecting our refilled extinguisher. I was just going for it. Let's hope we don't need it." The others had stopped to stare at the old man. He was wearing a brown fur vest and making sure his jacket swung open wide enough for it to be plainly seen.

"What a beautiful vest!" exclaimed Mrs. Pallant. "Where on earth did you find such an unusual one?"

"Oh, it's just one from my collection," murmured the seadog. "I've got so many I forget where half of them came from."

"It sure is a special one," put in the skipper. Then, turning to the others, he said, "I'll leave you all to finish while I arrange with the boatyard to keep an eye on our car and also let them know our float plan. Then we can push off."

When they had finished, the four crowded around the old man, eager to tell him how their plans had changed because of his instruction during the first trip. That pleased him considerably.

"Glad to have been of some help. Now, you will be leaving soon on your first voyage, so I'd better give you these now." He pulled four slim packages from his coat pocket and handed them one each.

"What are these?" they chorused.

"Open them and see!"

They quickly tore off the wrapping and gasped simultaneously.

Each was holding a well-used knife complete with leather sheath, polished by wear.

"Oh, boy!" exclaimed Harry. "A real sailor's knife!"

"That's right," nodded the old seadog. "They are from my collection."

"Collection?" Pauline queried.

"Yes. I've collected knives nearly all my life. I made a point of buying a new knife for each voyage, while the old one went into my collection, stamped with the name of the ship." Taking the knives one at a time, Spiff pointed the small markings—*Pamir, Valda, Mangela, San Pedro.*

"But Spiff," remonstrated Mrs. Pallant. "You shouldn't break up a collection like that. It's probably valuable, apart from the sentimental value."

"That's all right, Ma'am, I have a lot more. I want to give these youngsters something special as they are about to start their first real voyage. Sometimes a knife can save your life, or somebody else's, onboard a ship."

"Well, we certainly appreciate them," said Pete and there was a chorus of assent from the others.

"Mine looks like a pirate knife!" said Pauline proudly. "I wonder if it has ever been used to stab anybody!"

"Pauline!" exclaimed her mother. "Don't be so bloodthirsty!"

Everybody laughed, and then it all had to be explained to Mr. Pallant who had just returned. He too told the old man that his knife collection should not have been disturbed, but it was of no use.

"Off we go, then! Let's go forward, and push off as far as you can," he took his position behind the wheel. While the two boys rushed forward to do his bidding. Spiff gave a helping hand from the pier and then stood back to watch as the sleek boat pulled smoothly away.

"Goodbye Spiff!" called the skipper. "Thanks for the special gifts. See you in a few weeks." They all waved to the natty figure on the pier, and received a smart salute in return.

"I wish he was coming with us," remarked Harry.

"I'll wager he does too," said his uncle. "But I'm afraid there wouldn't be enough room for another one."

Pip lost no time in taking up his favorite position as far forward as possible, looking straight ahead.

"He must think he's a figurehead," observed Mrs. Pallant as she made herself comfortable near her husband.

The tide was on the ebb, so it was not long before they were clear of the channel and felt the boat lift to the ocean swell.

"Hoist the sails," called the skipper and the four youngsters leapt to their tasks like old-timers. They were all dressed in white shirts, with blue jeans rolled up to just below the knee and wearing the prized sheath knives at their belts. Bright-eyed and well-tanned, even to their bare feet, they made a smart crew, and the skipper was quick to notice it.

"Well done!" he said when they had finished. "Not only did you act like real sailors, but you even look the part!"

The four exchanged satisfied glances and Harry felt particularly pleased. "Now we are really sailing," he remarked, gazing with awe at the white canvas towering above.

"Sniff that breeze," said Pauline, and they all breathed deep of the pure air.

"What time do we eat?" asked Wendy suddenly.

Her mother laughed. "Well, it's two hours since your last meal, so I suppose you must be hungry! You can get something for all of us if you like."

Wendy thought for a moment. "No thanks, I'm not that hungry!"

"While we are on the subject," put in her father. "Don't forget what I said about the cooking. Your mother is the first mate, not the cook, so we will all take turns to act as cook."

"How will we know what to cook?" asked Pauline.

"The duty cook will have free hand to choose and prepare the meal." Her father looked around at the solemn faces of the four and had to laugh. "Well, it won't be that bad! Look on it as a challenge. There is an old saying that a good sea cook can always produce some kind of a meal, and if necessary, he can make a good soup out of practically anything, even an old dishcloth!"

"Well, I don't know anything about cooking," said Harry.

"Neither do I," added Pete. "Cooking is girl's work."

"Oh, no, it isn't," chorused his sisters.

"All the sea cooks I ever knew were men," put in the skipper.

"But if you want to make it easier, Harry and Pauline can work together, and then Wendy and Pete.

"Good!" Wendy said. "We'll show 'em, Pete!"

"That's settled then," the skipper decided.

Shortly afterwards, the breeze freshened more and backed more to the east, changing the situation completely as far as sailing was concerned. Now, in order to make headway, the *Seawolf* had to sail on short port and starboard tracks alternately and this meant that the four were kept almost continuously busy handling sheets and dodging the swinging boom. They were more than relieved when the wind veered again a couple of hours later and allowed the schooner to maintain a steady course.

"That's all for now," called out the skipper. "You all did very well."

"Phew!" gasped Wendy, flopping full length on the cabin roof. "I'm bushed. Now I come to think of it, I don't remember ever saying that I wanted to be a sailor!"

"I certainly didn't," declared Pauline as she collapsed near her sister. "It's really hard work. I imagined all you had to do on a boat was sit in the deckchair and watch the waves go by!"

The boys were just as glad to rest, but they had barely settled down near the girls when Pete exclaimed, "Oh, Mom!"

The others sat up just in time to see Mrs. Pallant arrive with a tray holding a large jug of lemonade and some glasses. "I think you really earned this," she smiled as she filled the glasses.

"Don't forget the poor helmsman!" put in her husband.

The next hour passed pleasantly as everybody relaxed. The *Seawolf* was heeled over by the pressure of the wind in her sails, but everybody, including Pip, was quickly getting used to moving around on a sloping deck.

"I'm hungry," announced Pauline suddenly.

"I've been waiting for that," smiled her father. "Awa-a-a-ay sea cooks, Wendy and Pete!"

Pete pulled himself upright with a groan and followed Wendy down into the cockpit, "What would you like to eat, Mom?" he asked.

"That is entirely up to you two. You dish up a tasty meal and we'll eat it," his mother answered cheerfully.

"And the sooner the better," called Pauline from where she was sprawled in the shade of the mainsail.

"What shall we cook, Pete?" asked Wendy as they squeezed into the tiny galley amidships.

"We have a free hand, so it's easy," he replied. "You prepare a large pile of bread and butter and leave the rest to me. I can cook a little. Where is the can opener?"

"Good for you, Pete," exclaimed Wendy as she watched him open six large cans. "Let's have plenty."

Twenty minutes later the two cooks staggered on deck, each carrying a tray holding three large plates piled high and steaming hot.

"That smells good," declared their mother. "What is it?" Then as she got a closer look, she exclaimed, "Good Heavens!"

"Ye Gods!" said her husband as he received his plate. "Is this a meal? Half a ton of piping hot baked beans in tomato sauce, with a frozen tomato sitting on top?"

Pete looked surprised. "We like baked beans, but I did only one can each because the plates wouldn't hold any more. If you can't eat them I will. I put the tomato on top because Mom is always on to us to eat plenty of salad stuff."

His mother was trying not to laugh. "And this is all we get?" she asked.

"No, of course not," said Wendy. "There's piles of bread and butter."

Pauline's eyes lit up when she saw her plate was almost overflowing. "This is what I call a decent meal," she gurgled. "I vote Pete and Wendy do all the cooking!"

"I think not," declared the skipper as he separated about a sixth of the beans on his plate. "I vote that they be demoted to deck swabbers for the rest of the voyage."

"Well, we like this meal," asserted Wendy. "But we don't mind not having to do any more cooking. Do we Pete?"

"Not at all!" grinned her brother as he shoveled up his beans. "You can't please grown-ups anyway."

"Well, the other two can have a try at supper-time," declared his father. "Maybe they'll show a little more imagination."

After lunch they all took turns at the wheel under the watchful eye and patient guidance of the skipper. Then he took the wheel himself again. "Better than I dared hope," he announced. "You all seem to be natural sailors, and before we get back home, I expect you will all be able to handle the boat as good as I can."

The *Seawolf* was now surging along as though she was alive and thoroughly enjoying her natural element.

"She's going like a thoroughbred," said Mr. Pallant proudly. "Eight knots and not even straining."

*Bertram Smith*

# Chapter Seven

## *SEA SOUP!*

The afternoon sun was hot, so the four relaxed in the shade of the sails for next hour or two. They were brought back to life when the skipper announced he would like a relief at the wheel. Both boys immediately volunteered and Harry was thrilled when he was chosen.

"You will get plenty of opportunity later, Pete," explained his father. "After Harry's vacation is over. Anyhow, I have another job for you. Your sisters can help too, if they wish."

"No thanks," said Pauline. "I am doing just fine."

"What is the job?" Pete asked cautiously.

"These decks are too hot, and I'm afraid the caulking will become loose," replied the skipper. "So get to work with a bucket and sluice them down. You get the bucket and I'll show you how to attach the line to it and haul up seawater without being pulled overboard."

Selecting a short length of light line, he demonstrated how to hitch it to a bucket handle so that it could not slip, and then showed how a bucket should be dropped overboard upside down and then jerked upright to fill it before swinging it back onboard.

Pete soon got the hang of it and began sluicing the side decks with a will. "Aren't you two going to help?" he asked his sisters who were still taking it easy on the cabin top.

"You don't need any help," said Wendy. "I never saw anybody do such a fine job!"

"You didn't, eh?" her brother queried. "Well, it seems to me that this cabin roof is too hot, and I might as well—"

As he spoke, he poured a bucket of water gently over the top of the cabin so that it would spread slowly under his sisters. But they were too quick for him. Grabbing the boom overhead, they managed to pull themselves up enough for the water to pass harmlessly under them.

"Missed!" chortled Wendy as she and her sister swung themselves to the deck on the far side.

Before Pete could think of anything else, his father spoke up. "As you girls are on your feet, you may as well give the deck a scrub. You'll find two long-handled scrubbers in the forepeak."

"I've read about ships like this," said Pauline darkly. "Working the crews until they drop."

"And without pay," added her sister as she reluctantly selected a scrubber.

A bucket of cold seawater sloshed around their ankles made the girls get a move on, and soon they were in the middle of a water fight amid gales of laughter.

By the time the job was finished and they had dried themselves, it was supper-time.

"What shall we have for supper?" asked Pauline.

"You decide," said her mother.

"How about cold meat and salad?" asked Harry, who knew his limitation as a cook.

"And some soup," put in Pauline quickly.

"That will do fine," said her father. "Go to it."

The two duty cooks made their way below. "I'll take care of the soup," said Pauline. "I have something special in mind."

"O.K." agreed her cousin. "I can manage the meat and salad. I'll prepare it on the cabin table and leave the galley to you."

Twenty minutes later, Pauline called out, "Do you particularly want soup Harry?"

"I can take it or leave it. Why?"

"Well, there happens to be only enough for four."

She emerged from the galley carefully balancing a tray with two steaming dishes on it. "Will you bring the other tray for Pete and Wendy?" Harry collected the other tray and followed his cousin out on deck.

"Ah!" exclaimed the skipper. "Thin soup, eh? That's my favorite. What kind is it?"

"Er—sea soup," replied Pauline, staring into space.

"Sea soup?" queried her mother looking at it closely. "It seems to have a peculiar smell. What did you put into it?"

Her husband was taking a sip as she spoke. "Pah!" he exclaimed and quickly spat it overboard. "What the heck is this made from? It tastes awful!" He shuddered and stared at his plate. "It's salty, too," he added.

"Well, it was your suggestion," said Pauline, apparently having some trouble keeping a straight face.

Her father stared at her suspiciously. "My suggestion? What did I suggest?"

"You said a good sea cook could make a tasty soup out of an old dishrag, so I thought I'd try it!"

"Pauline!" gasped her mother. "You mean you just boiled a dish cloth in ordinary water?"

"Of course not. That would probably have been tasteless."

"Well, what did you use?" choked her father. "Bilgewater?"

"No. I never thought of that. I used seawater, but I suppose I shouldn't have added more salt."

For a moment it seemed as though her father was going to explode, judging by his purple face, and Pauline started to back off. Then he let out a roar, but to her vast relief, it was of laughter.

"All right! You win!" he gasped, wiping his eyes. "That was just a humorous saying I quoted about sea cooks, as you well knew, and I suspect you are the only person in the world who has actually tried to do it."

Everybody joined in the laughter as all the plates of soup were tipped overboard. "I hope the meat and salad are all right," said Mrs. Pallant anxiously.

"Oh, they are," Harry assured her. "I took care of them while Pauline concentrated on the soup."

"I'll wager she really did concentrate," remarked his uncle. "Only Pauline could think up a scheme like that."

After supper, they all relaxed on deck and enjoyed the glory of the sunset as the sinking sun painted the sky astern.

"Look at the sails," exclaimed Wendy suddenly. "They look as though they are on fire."

The red rays of the dying sun had now caught the sails, bathing them in a crimson glow, and everybody gazed in awe at the fiery splendor. "What a picture," murmured the skipper. "This can happen only at sea." A few moments later the glow faded and they were back on an ordinary schooner once again.

Dusk followed quickly and the skipper switched on the red and green navigation lights. Almost at once, it seemed, the sky was full of stars.

"The sails seem even bigger in the dark," observed Harry as he watched the topmasts weaving gently back and forth against the starry background.

"Most things appear larger and also closer in the dark than they actually are," observed his uncle. "Which is an advantage when you are piloting. Incidentally, can any of you identify the Pole Star?"

"I don't see how anybody can pick out a particular star when the sky is so full," said Pete.

"It's not so difficult," his father declared and then went on to explain how the better-known stars can be located. The four listened with rapt attention, and he would probably have given them a lengthy lecture on astronomy had not his wife intervened.

"I think it is about time some people were in bed," she put in.

"Oh, not on a night like this," protested Pauline. "There's no school or anything tomorrow."

"Thank Heaven for that!" chuckled Wendy. "What time do we have to get up tomorrow morning, anyhow?"

"Well, we are sailing all night," said her father, "but as this is your first night at sea you can all spend it in bed. Your mother is staying up with me for a while and then I'll carry on alone until about four o'clock. Pete and Harry can take over at that time and have the watch until eight. We should be off Seal Island by then and we will have to change course. I will put her on the new course before I go off watch."

Pete's face reflected his feelings. "Four o'clock? I thought you said that we can spend all night in bed?"

"That's right—until four o'clock," replied the skipper with a wide grin.

The four trooped below and Harry chuckled to himself as he heard Pete muttering something about it paying to be a girl because then you could spend half your life in bed! Switching on the lights, they drew the curtains across the short passage joining the two cabins and it was not long before they were all ready for bed.

"This is comfortable," sighed Pauline as she snuggled down in her settee bed. Then she noticed that her sister was tense and quiet. "Wendy, what are you doing with that piece of–?"

"Shh!" hissed Wendy. She was listening intently with a wicked grin on her face. "Peter," she called softly through the curtains. "Are you in bed, yet?"

"I just got in, and I'm not getting out for anything. What do you want?"

"Good!" she whispered. A second later, there was a crash followed by a howl from Peter.

"What on earth happened?" demanded Pauline and Harry together.

Mrs. Pallant put her head in the doorway and demanded, "What's going on?"

"I don't know," replied Pete, rubbing his head. "I was just settling down when all these books suddenly jumped off this little shelf and onto my head. Did the boat roll or something?"

"No, it did not," she replied tersely. "Now, stop playing around or I'll send your father down." She withdrew, leaving Pete feeling his head carefully for bumps.

"How could that happen?" he wondered. Sitting up, he examined the bookshelf. "Books and things don't just jump off shelves on their own." Groping around, he suddenly exclaimed, "Ah, ha! There's a piece of string here. One end is tied to the shelf and I guess it ran behind the books. I wonder where the other end is—as if I didn't know."

He traced the string to where it disappeared behind the bulkhead and then gave it a sudden jerk, causing Wendy to let out a squeal of pent-up laughter.

"I thought so," said Pete grimly. "Wendy, I'm going to—" but he couldn't wait to explain. He made a dive straight from his bed towards the curtain across the passageway, exactly as Wendy expected him to. As soon as she saw the shape of his head bulge the curtain, she swung a cushion hard, and her brother shot back into his own cabin with a crash. He gave a yell when his head struck the end of the table, but it was immediately drowned by a roar from his father.

"Pipe down below there, or by thunder, I'll come down with a rope's end and tan the lot of you!"

Harry was half out of bed on his way to help Pete, but he shot back like a scared rabbit. "Golly! Isn't he fierce?" he gasped.

"Oh, he's a monster, sometimes," said Wendy mischievously.

"No, he's not," declared Pauline.

"Of course he isn't," said Pete as he rubbed his head. "He just likes to roar sometimes. If ever he did any of the things he promises, we would probably suffer from shock as much as anything else! However, we'd better be quiet now. I am going to have a lovely dream about what I am going to do to get even with Wendy. I don't suppose you have any thumbtacks handy, do you?"

"Thumbtacks?" Harry stared at his cousin. "What the heck do you want thumbtacks for?"

"I want to pin Wendy's ears to the main mast just to start!"

Harry had to stuff the sheet into his mouth to stifle his laughter as he visualised Wendy dangling by her ears from the mast. There were muffled giggles coming from the other cabin, then a click as the light was switched off. Still muttering to himself, Pete turned off their light, and all was quiet at last.

Harry stretched himself luxuriously on the comfortable settee and listened to the gentle swish of water moving past the outside of the hull, broken by the occasional creak of timbers. From above, the straining of ropes and canvas hummed a soothing lullaby and he could feel the gentle rise and fall of the boat, with just a hint of a roll. *How different from the farm,* he told himself drowsily. *Sleeping on a boat is even better than I imagined.*

The wind held steady as the *Seawolf* sailed on through the darkness. Occasionally the lights of other ships appeared in the distance, but none came close. Mrs. Pallant was still with her husband at the wheel when the Seal Island light loomed over the horizon on the port bow, and they watched it draw steadily nearer. It was past four o'clock before the change of course could be made safely, and the skipper was yawning widely by the time it was done.

"Take the wheel for a few minutes, Ivy," he said. "So I can call the watch."

"It's a pity to disturb them," she remarked as she took his place.

"It is. But we have a long way to go and I must have a few hours sleep." He was stretching as he spoke and then began feeling his way into the dark cabin, with the intention of quietly waking the two boys.

As he entered, he stepped on something soft just inside, whereupon the quiet was immediately shattered by a sharp yelp followed by a growl. Something shot between his legs, causing him to lose his balance and sit down with a crash.

"What in thunder—?" he began as another growl came out of the darkness, "That darned dog!"

Both cabin lights snapped on.

"What happened, Dad?" Pete asked.

"I must have stepped on Pip. The last time I saw him he was on the foredeck, and I must have assumed he was sleeping there, without really thinking about it. Never mind, Pip!" he added, rubbing the dog's head as Pip started to lick his face.

Scrambling to his feet, the skipper said briskly, "Watch on deck, please take over. Keep her as she is going now, but call me if the wind changes."

"Aye-aye, Sir," responded Pete smartly. "Come along, Harry."

The boys dressed quickly and made their way on deck where Pete took over the wheel from his mother. Soon the boat was all quiet again as the two boys stood together at the wheel, feeling the cool breeze on their faces and breathing deeply of the salt air.

With the aid of the faint light over the compass, they could see that the course was now northeast. A three-quarter moon was riding high in the sky and bathing the whole starboard side of the boat and sails with pale light, while leaving the port side in deep shadow.

"That looks a little weird," remarked Pete. "But I suppose sailors get used to such things."

Harry gave a tremendous yawn. "Ghostly, is the word for it. What are those lights over yonder?"

"Ships," replied his cousin. "You can tell which way they are headed by the lights."

"I can?" Harry was surprised. "How?"

"If you see only the red or green lights, a ship must be passing one way or the other, but if you see both at the same time, the ships must be coming towards you."

"That's interesting. What shall we do if one comes close?"

"Nothing," replied Pete. "Steam must give way to sail, so they have to keep clear of us. Anyway, all those ships are passing a long way off, so we don't have to worry."

"Good. All we have to do is try to stay awake!"

"And keep on course," Pete applied a little pressure on the wheel. "You keep a lookout while I steer."

Twenty minutes later, Harry reported: "There's a ship coming straight for us."

"Yes, I see it. I hope they can see us."

The ship approached steadily and soon they were able to make out the faint outline of the masts, bridge, and funnel. A few dim lights showed on deck, but there was no sign of life. Still the ship held on course and speed, direct for the *Seawolf.*

"What shall we do, Pete?!" demanded Harry excitedly.

*Bertram Smith*

# Chapter Eight

## A CLOSE CALL.

Peter gasped as the ship loomed suddenly close.

"Better call Dad—" he began when a deep voice high up on the ship boomed out, clear and urgent: "Sailing boat ahead! Hard starboard!"

"Hard starboard," repeated another on the bridge and slowly the huge bow swung away. The ship cleared the *Seawolf* by only a few yards, taking all the wind out of her sails, and the two boys gazed in awe as the cliff-like side of a big freighter slid by. They heard the steady thump of her engine and propeller, and then they were rocking in her wake.

"Phew! That was a close call!" exclaimed Pete. "I wonder what Dad will say."

"Did we do something wrong?" asked Harry wonderingly.

"I don't think so. But that wouldn't have been much help if we had been run down. Didn't it seem a giant ship in the dark?"

"It sure did," agreed Harry. "And it seemed to be moving awfully fast. Thank goodness it will be daylight soon."

Dawn was no long in coming and soon they were enjoying the splendor of sunrise at sea. Daylight revealed a calm, almost empty sea, with the *Seawolf* practically steering herself in a steady breeze.

Taking turns at the wheel, the boys were so absorbed they were surprised when the skipper quietly emerged from the cabin, lit his pipe and announced that it was eight o'clock.

"What of the night, boys?" he asked as he took over the wheel, automatically checking the compass course as he did so.

"Fine," replied Pete. "Except for one thing."

"Oh?"

"A big freighter nearly ran us down!"

The pipe almost fell from his father's mouth. "What? Why didn't you call me?"

Peter described exactly what happened. The skipper listened carefully and then said: "Well, you did have the right of way, but there is a provision in the Rules of the Road at Sea which requires every vessel to take any action necessary to avoid a collision. You should have called me."

"We couldn't believe they would ignore us until the last moment," explained Harry. "And then the ship suddenly seemed to be on top of us."

"I don't suppose they were ignoring you," replied his uncle. "Although it is possible that the lookout man was dozing. He should have seen our lights in plenty of time to change course. However, it's over and done with. You two can take it easy now."

At that moment, the mate emerged from the cabin with four steaming cups of coffee and some cookies. "Come on, you sailors," she said. "I expect you can do with some hot coffee. The girls are still asleep, so they can have some later."

While they were sipping their coffee, Pete drew his cousin to one side. "Did you hear that? The girls are still sleeping!"

Harry stared. "So what?"

"I've just got the idea I needed. Come and help me get a bucket of seawater down below without anybody seeing us."

"A bucket of seawater," repeated the other. "What on earth for?"

"You'll see. Come on!"

While his parents were talking at the wheel, Pete took a bucket from a locker and dipped it quickly over the lee side and handed it down the forehatch to Harry. Following, he took the bucket and stole silently into the cabin where the girls were sleeping. Placing the bucket carefully in position, he then shook Wendy by the shoulder and whispered urgently: "Wendy! We are passing and iceberg. It looks so cold. Come on deck quickly and see it!"

He slipped back to rejoin his cousin in the other cabin and they heard Wendy murmur, "Cold iceberg," sleepily as she swung her feet out of bed.

A split second later the early morning peace was shattered by a bloodcurdling scream from Wendy which caused several things to happen at once. Pauline, being the nearest, got the full effect and she literally shot out of bed and onto her feet before waking. Pip, asleep on his back, started to bark while struggling desperately to get to his feet.

Mrs. Pallant gasped, "That was Wendy!" and rushed down below, past the startled boys and into the other cabin. "Whatever is the matter?"

Wendy was sitting on her bed, clutching her feet and half sobbing with rage. "Somebody—and I know who—put a bucket of cold water just where my feet go when I get out of bed, and then woke me up with some story about passing an iceberg. Ugh! For a moment, I thought I'd put my feet on it!"

Her mother repressed a smile. "I suppose it was Pete up to his tricks again. I'll speak to him about it, although I expect you played some other trick on him."

"Come on!" whispered Pete to his cousin. "Let's go!" He led the way on deck looking as casual as he could. His father glanced at them as they emerged. "What happened?"

Pete put on his most innocent look. "I heard Wendy telling Mom something about an iceberg and cold water. Maybe she had a dream."

"I wouldn't be surprised if you were involved somehow," remarked the skipper suspiciously.

"He was!" His wife spoke from the cabin doorway. "And if he plays any more fancy tricks like that, I'll stick his head in a bucket of icy water!"

She explained to her husband what had happened while the two boys wandered casually forward, as far as they could get.

A little later, the four sat down to breakfast and Wendy glowered at her brother. "That was a nasty thing to do. But don't worry. I'll think of something just as bad to do to you!"

Pete pretended surprise. "What makes you think I had anything to do with it? You know how you are for dreaming."

"I know!" said Wendy emphatically. "And I know that you know what I know."

"Well, it seems to me to be more like an abstract, visionary creation of the imagination," Pete spoke the words carefully.

Pauline rolled her eyes in pretend agony. "Listen to them, Harry. Aren't you glad you are an only child?"

"It sounds as though Pete has been at his dictionary again," sighed Wendy. "Don't tell me you even brought it along on vacation."

"Of course I did," replied her brother virtuously. "I have to think of my education!" Winking at Harry, he went on, "I like to glance at it occasionally and then, next day at school, I try a few new words on my English teacher. It seems to make him think I have been hitting my homework especially hard, and that makes him feel good!"

"You mean Old Kipper Feet," said Pauline.

Harry looked around the table. "Here we go again," he said. "How could anybody possibly have a name like 'Kipper Feet'?"

"Simple," grinned Pauline. "He is wide without being fat, and he walks like you imagine a kipper would walk—if a kipper could!"

"It doesn't sound simple to me," Harry said. "All the teachers at my school are ordinary people with ordinary names."

"How boring," put in Wendy, already restored to her usual self.

After breakfast, the boys relieved the skipper at the wheel so that he could eat and also check his navigation. Soon after he went below, the weather began to deteriorate and a freshening breeze soon created a choppy sea. The *Seawolf* was beginning to feel it by the time the skipper returned to the deck, and he scanned the sky carefully.

"I don't like the look of those clouds," he remarked. "I hope the weather isn't going to break up. We've had a wonderful run so far and I was hoping to carry the fine weather with us all the way."

Soon the strengthening wind drove the waves into whitecaps and the schooner heeled over until her lee rail was awash, while her bows began to rise and fall sharply.

Everybody except Pip was on deck by this time and holding on tightly to rails or rigging. "This really is sailing!" cried Pauline as she ducked to avoid the slashing spray. "Is it going to get really rough?"

"I hope not," replied her father. "It doesn't look too serious yet. We are really making some speed now, though."

"When do you expect to arrive?" The mate was having difficulty making herself heard above the wind.

"If we keep going like this, we should reach Halifax by tomorrow afternoon. Meanwhile, I hope Pip is all right."

"He's safe on my settee," said Pauline. "He has more sense than to come out in weather like this!"

As the day wore on, the wind showed no signs of easing and the seas had built up enough to make the schooner plunge heavily. One moment her bows were pointing skyward and the next she was burying them in the emerald ocean. This sent heavy sheets of spray slicing across the deck; eventually, the skipper decided to shorten sail. This needed all hands and it proved to be exciting trying to keep a foothold on wet, slippery decks which did not keep still for very long. But the job was accomplished in good time and then the *Seawolf* rode easier, with little loss of speed.

Cooking was out of the question on the stove which sloped badly as well as rising and falling sharply, so Mrs. Pallant prepared a cold lunch with the aid of the girls. It was a difficult job in cramped, bouncing quarters, especially as they always needed one hand to hold on with. Then they had fun trying to eat from a table which rolled and lurched around like a bronco, making dishes slide in all directions.

During the afternoon the two boys took over the wheel to allow the skipper to consult his chart. The boat was now plunging and yawing so much that it required their combined strength to hold her steady.

"We are doing fine," the skipper announced when he returned. "By dusk we should be able to swing towards the north. That will put the seas behind us and make her ride easier."

The *Seawolf* plowed steadily on with green seas curling along her lee deck, but holding her course and speed like a veteran. Soon the sun took refuge behind ragged clouds and dusk came on early. It was another hour though, before the skipper was able to ease the helm a little. As they came slowly around on the new course the heavy plunging and surging diminished, allowing the *Seawolf* to assume a more upright position, making life easier for everybody. Even Pip showed his face on deck to see what was happening.

Supper was a more comfortable affair, and as the evening drew on, the skipper announced that the ladies could now take over for a spell while the men took a well-earned break. "You run the ship until nine p.m.," he said. "The boys can take over until midnight, and I will take the rest of the night."

"Good!" sighed Pete. "I'm practically worn out!"

"O.K." said his mother, pulling her peaked cap firmly into position. "We can do it. Girls, I want you to act as lookouts—one on each side. I will take the wheel. Be sure to report any ships or boats coming to close."

"Aye-aye, Mom!" the girls chorused. "You can rely on us."

Their father had to chuckle. "I can see the ship is in good hands. Come on, fellers. You should have a nap, too. You didn't have much sleep last night."

During the evening, the weather began to clear and the sea gradually calmed down. By the time the skipper came on deck at midnight, it was a beautiful starry night presided over by a bright moon and he breathed deeply in appreciation.

Traffic was light and he was able to settle down for a quiet smoke at the wheel. He heard the boys preparing for bed and then the boat was quiet. Making himself comfortable, while keeping a good lookout, he was surprised when dawn began to lighten the eastern sky. Then, a little later, the mate appeared with a welcome cup of coffee. After a quiet chat with her husband, she went to prepare breakfast, glad to have a stable platform to work on.

During the forenoon, the skipper announced that they were now passing Lunenburg, birthplace of Bluenose, the most famous schooner of them all. Harry managed to get a turn with the binoculars and eagerly scanned the coast. "I'll bet pirates have often done this from here!" he remarked, as he swung the glasses ahead. Then he reported, "I can see a big headland in the distance on the port bow."

"That should be Sambro Head," said his uncle. "We have to leave that to port as we turn towards Halifax harbor. Only another twenty miles or so after that."

Lunch was over and the helmsman relieved to allow him to get his, before the massive headland loomed close. Then it took another hour to sail around it before a course could be set for the big harbor at Halifax. "Now boys," said the skipper. "This is the time to use one of the signal halyards you rove. Which one of you rigged the foremast?"

"I did," said Harry proudly.

"Fine. Then you get to use it first. When entering a foreign port, it is customary to fly the flag of that country at the fore masthead as a courtesy, in addition to flying your own at the sternstaff. So, Pete, you help Harry find the Maple Leaf flag in the locker and then hoist it."

It did not take long to find the distinctive Canadian flag, but Harry had to be shown how to secure it to the halyard. Then he hoisted it carefully and soon it was fluttering proudly at the truck of the foremast. It seemed a long way from the deck.

They were now in a busy traffic lane and passing vessels of all kinds, some inbound like themselves, but mostly outbound. A rusty freighter passed close by, followed by an equally neglected tanker, and then came the sparkling white cruise ship. The four gazed up in awe as the floating palace slid by. Passengers lined every available railing and most of them seemed to be looking down at the *Seawolf*. Probably excited at the beginning of their voyage, many waved cheerfully and the four returned the waves with gusto.

Later on, the skipper remarked, "All this traffic is making me nervous. I need more control, so I think I'll take her in from here by motor. Start her up, Pete, and the rest of you stand by to drop the sails."

The engine started at first try and the sails came down smartly. They were soon furled and then the crew relaxed again.

"What kind of ship is that coming up from behind?" asked Harry a little later.

The skipper glanced over his shoulder. "It's the Canadian Navy. A light cruiser, no less. Take the wheel, Ivy, so that I can stand by to dip the ensign."

The lean, gray shape of the Canadian warship was rapidly overtaking them on the port side, and as it drew close, they could see the long lines of the white-uniformed seamen paraded along the foredeck.

"Look!" exclaimed Pete. "See how all the sailors are lined up for entering port? Why don't we try that? Let's show them how smart we can be!"

Scrambling quickly, the four lined up on the foredeck of the *Seawolf* facing the warship. As it drew abreast, the skipper dipped his ensign in the international salute and, simultaneously, a seaman at the stern of the cruiser dipped the Canadian ensign. The four stood ramrod straight watching the big ship move slowly past. They saw the captain stroll over to the wing of his bridge and look down. He appeared to run a critical eye over the trim schooner, from the man securing the ensign at the stern to the woman capably steering, and then forward to the four youngsters standing rigidly at attention. Evidently, he liked what he saw, because his tanned face lit up with a smile and he slowly raised his right hand to the peak of his cap in a salute especially for them.

"Shall we salute back?" whispered Pauline.

"Don't move!" hissed Pete.

Then the cruiser seemed to leave them quickly behind.

"Well done, you four," called the skipper as he returned to the wheel. "I think we all did our bit to strengthen international relations today! I've always had a lot of respect for the Canadian Navy."

"Me too!" exclaimed his wife, her eyes misty with pride.

"Well, it sure made me feel proud for some reason," put in Harry, whose eyes were misty too.

Ahead, a massive bridge came into view. Arching across the harbor entrance, it made an impressive sight against the blue sky and the four studied it with awe.

"That is Angus MacDonald Bridge," the skipper told them. "You can see how high it is, and yet, when we sail underneath it, it will appear as though our masts are too tall to pass under safely. Watch!"

Sure enough, as the *Seawolf* began to pass under the arch, it did appear as though the mastheads must strike it. And yet, when it was actually towering above them, there was obviously much more than enough room.

"You might call that an optical illusion," said the skipper, "Because there is a hundred and sixty feet clear! There is another big bridge at the far end of the harbor, but we won't have to go that far. We should be able to find a berth somewhere around here. I'll pull alongside the Customs Office and find out what is available. By the time we get moored it will be suppertime, and after that, we will find out about contacting Anita."

An hour later, they had cleared customs and secured the *Seawolf* in a safe berth. Supper did not take long and then Mrs. Pallant announced: "Now we will get ready to go ashore, and I think a little smartening up is called for. After all, we are going into a city and we don't want to be mistaken for a bunch of tramps."

There was a scramble to find suitable going ashore outfits.

"I'm looking forward to showing Anita my knife," remarked Pauline.

"I'm afraid not," put in her father. All four looked at him in surprise as he went on: "A sheath knife is very useful onboard, but ashore it can be regarded as a concealed weapon. And carrying a concealed weapon is against the law. Why not wait until Anita comes sailing with us and then surprise her? I'm sure she will also be surprised when she sees how well you handle yourselves when we are under way."

"Is Pip coming?" asked Wendy.

"He must stay onboard and guard the boat. We don't know this place, so we won't risk leaving an unguarded boat, even for a few hours."

*Bertram Smith*

# Chapter Nine

## *THE STORY OF THE TREASURE.*

A taxi deposited them at a modern apartment building in the city and soon the family greetings were in full swing. Harry had wondered what a sister of the triplets would be like. He found her to be a self-possessed young woman, slim and dark-haired like her mother, and with the Pallant sense of humor always bubbling near the surface.

"Glad to meet you, Harry," she said as she shook his hand. "How do you find life with the triplets? A little wearing?"

"We get along just fine," Harry smiled sincerely.

"Oh, they are not a bad bunch, just a little weird at times, I suppose!" Anita grinned.

When Mrs. Pallant had duly admired her daughter's furnishings, and they were all settled down, Anita said: "Dad, did you ever hear of the Oak Island Treasure?"

"Oh, yes," he replied. "As you know, I've always been very interested in lost treasure and wrecks at one time. I remember the Oak Island case because it was such an unusual story. Why do you ask?"

"Because there is a short piece in the local newspaper about it, which I think might interest you." She noticed the sudden close interest the four youngsters were giving her and she had to laugh. "I suppose I had better read it aloud!"

Pulling the small clipping from her purse, Anita read: "Two engineers, who recently purchased the right to search for the Oak Island treasure, have been at work with modern equipment and they now claim to have finally located the treasure chamber. They expect to be able to get the treasure out within a few days. Meanwhile, no one is allowed on the island."

"Good luck to them," Mr. Pallant said. "They may manage it, but a lot of other people have tried in the past."

Harry found it difficult to contain himself. The very thought of buried treasure made him feel excited, and yet, this family was discussing it as though it was nothing unusual.

"Where is this Oak Island?" he asked of anybody who might listen.

"We passed it yesterday," the skipper said casually.

"*What?!*" the triplets sat up and spoke as one.

"I don't remember seeing it," said Pete.

"You didn't," agreed his father. "It is in Mahone Bay and we were twenty miles out at sea!"

"Mahone Bay?" queried Anita. "Then I suppose you know about the ghost ship there too!"

The four youngsters exchanged glances—speechless for once.

The skipper looked surprised. "No, I don't know anything about that. Where did you hear of it?"

"I came across it in the local library when I was looking for something else, and I made a note in case you hadn't heard about it—although I didn't think that was very likely! Here it is," she opened her notebook and read:

*"A famous story of Mahone Bay is that of the American Privateer Young Teazer. In 1813 she was chased into the bay by a British Man-O-War and burst into flames. Since then, numerous witnesses have reported ghostly appearances of this ship. Sometimes she appears as her normal self, and at others, she is a ball of fire, flaring on and off. According to legend, the appearance always precedes a storm."*

There was a short silence, which Pauline was the first to break. "Well, I never thought my father would take us past treasure islands and ghost ships without even telling us!"

Her father laughed at such exasperation and Harry took the opportunity to ask, "Am I the only one that doesn't know the story of the Oak Island Treasure?"

"No!" cried the triplets in unison.

"And it's cruelty not to tell us!" added Wendy slyly.

"All right, I don't mind repeating it, if everybody wants to hear it." Apparently, everybody did, so the skipper began:

"Nobody knows for sure, but the legend is that Captain Kidd, the notorious pirate, buried his treasure cache on Oak Island during the late 1700's. Whomever did bury it made sure that it wouldn't be found and removed easily. As I remember it, the whole thing was started in the early 1800's by three boys while on a canoe trip from the mainland. They had all decided to explore the island and while doing so, sat down under a lone oak tree for a rest. They soon noticed a depression in the ground some ten feet square and apparently man-made. Although now well overgrown with grass, it looked as though a big hole might have been dug there at some time.

"Then one of the boys pointed at a large branch of the tree which was directly over the depression. It was badly chafed and worn as though some kind of tackle had been secured to it. After some discussion, they decided that something heavy could have been buried under the tree and, having heard tales of buried treasure, the three concocted a plan to dig under the tree without telling anybody about it."

"Can't you just imagine it?" asked Harry dreamily. "We would probably have done the same!"

The other three murmured assent as the skipper continued:

"They returned the next day with shovels and a pickaxe and set to work with a will. An hour or two later, they were about to give up in disgust when they struck wood. Excited, they quickly cleared it, probably expecting some kind of treasure chest, but it turned out to be a platform of oak planks, about ten feet down.

"It is easy to imagine the disappointment at this find. But it was also exciting, because the platform had obviously been put there for a reason, and it seemed pretty certain that there must be something hidden below it.

"After more hard digging, they struck wood again at about twenty feet, but it proved to be another oak platform. Tired and reluctant to give up, they had to admit that it was as far as they could go without help, so gradually, their parents and more and more people came into the picture.

"Equipment was taken out to the island and the pit deepened, but at every ten feet, another barrier was found, either of planks or a hard putty-like material. At ninety feet the shovels struck stone and a flat tablet was unearthed with some words carved into it. Pausing to clear the letters, the diggers must have been stunned when they read the words:

### *'Forty feet below, ten million pounds lie buried'*

The weariest searchers would be spurred on by such a message, but when they struck an extensive stone barrier at one hundred feet, they probably believed it was the top of some kind of treasure chamber.

"At this point, work had to be stopped for the night, and what was expected to be the final effort was planned for early the next morning. But the first man on the job at dawn raised the alarm. During the night, the deep shaft had half filled with water!

"Bailers were put to work, and then pumps brought in, but although they kept at it for days, the water level never went down more than a few feet, only to rise again when they stopped. Finally, they gave up in disgust.

"Since then, many attempts have been made to locate the treasure, but the searchers have always been beaten by that water trap. Eventually, someone found that the water in the trap was salty, which meant that there was probably an underground tunnel connecting it to the sea. After much searching, a fan-shaped entrance with five arms was found among the rocks on the shore nearest to the pit. It was assumed that these drained into a central tunnel which led to the treasure shaft and attempts were made to locate this by drilling, but without success.

"Later on, somebody thought of putting red dye into the shaft in the hope that the colored water would emerge from the main intake. He must have been surprised when none showed up, and really surprised when he heard that colored water had appeared on the opposite side of the island! This meant that there must be more than one entrance to the tunnels guarding the treasure.

"So, the years have gone by with people trying and failing to locate that treasure, until the vicinity of the original shaft became honeycombed with excavations and cluttered with abandoned gear. The cost of all this searching must have totaled a fabulous amount."

There was silence in the room for a moment. Everybody was fascinated by the story, but Harry remained puzzled. "But is there any real proof that there is treasure down there?"

"It was proved some years ago," replied his uncle. "An engineer put a small drill down through the roof of the treasure chamber and brought up a piece, just a tiny piece of a gold chain, and a fragment of parchment.

"World War Two interrupted the treasure hunting, but it has built up again steadily since then, and almost every summer someone else wants to have a try. The latest is these two engineers who claim, as many have before, that they will soon have the treasure out. They seem to be very sure of themselves, so maybe this will be the end of a very long treasure hunt."

"Let's go there!" urged Pauline, her eyes shining. "Maybe we will be able to see the treasure!"

Her father smiled at her eagerness. "Well, if it really is located this time there will, no doubt, be lots of excitement, so it might be a good time to be the vicinity." He thought for a moment and then shook his head. "It wouldn't do much good though, nobody is allowed on the island."

"I would just love to see it brought up after so long," said Pete wistfully. "Imagine seeing a real pirate's treasure!"

"It really would be a thrill to be nearby if they do manage to get the treasure out after trying for so many years," said his mother thoughtfully. "Why can't we go?"

Her husband was a little taken aback from this attack from an unexpected quarter. "Well, you know I had planned on an easy day tomorrow after we had cleaned ship, but I suppose we can go to Mahone Bay if we want to. But don't plan on getting shore."

"It would be a thrill just to see the island," put in Harry. "Stories of buried treasure are among my favorites and I've often wished I could see a real treasure island."

"All right, that's settled," announced the skipper. "We sail tomorrow morning for a modern treasure island! We can do the trip in a day, anchor for the night and return the next day, so we'll be away only one night. Can you come along, Anita?"

She shook her head regretfully. "I have a big meeting on tomorrow and, something I haven't been able to tell you about yet, I have started doing volunteer work for the police!"

"Good for you, Anita!" exclaimed her mother. "That should be really worthwhile. Two of my brothers were policemen and I have always been interested in police work. Maybe I should volunteer!"

"I am sure you would be welcome, Mom, and it really is interesting."

"What do you do?" Wendy wanted to know.

"Well, my next-door neighbor happens to be a sergeant in the Royal Canadian Mounted Police and when he found out that I am an artist, he asked if I could draw faces. I told him I can, so he asked me if I would care to do a little volunteer work for them, creating pictures of criminals from descriptions. I agreed to help and I go along two days a week. It's fascinating work, and already one of my drawings helped to catch a criminal! Also, I'm helping with an undercover operation, but I can't tell you anything about that yet!"

"That's wonderful, Anita!" said her father. "We are so proud of you! We look forward to hearing more about it when you're able to tell. Maybe you'll be able to come sailing with us next weekend. In the meantime, we'd better be off now. We have a busy day tomorrow."

"We love you, Anita!" her mother came in with a hug as everyone waved goodbye.

Three more of the biggest hugs from the triplets, my how they love their eldest sister.

Next morning at breakfast, the skipper announced, "I have to check my charts and figure out our new courses, so there will be time for you four to wash down before we leave. It is much easier here than when we are under way."

When the four went to collect buckets and scrubbers, an argument quickly developed over who would do the scrubbing and who would haul the water.

"We did the scrubbing last time!" said Pauline. "The boys should do it this time."

"Hauling water requires a certain knack which boys have naturally," responded Pete. "So let's get on with it."

"Listen to the new Captain," put in Pauline. "You know we can do anything you can do, and do it better!"

They were interrupted by a deep voice booming up through the skylight. "This is the old Captain speaking, and still in command. If you don't cut the cackle and get on with the job, I'll put you all to holystoning the decks!"

There was a sudden silence on deck. Then Wendy whispered: "Holystone? I've heard of holy orders and holy smoke, but what on earth is holystone?"

"It's a large, flat piece of sandstone used by sailors to scour decks and make them white," said Pete. "It's been around for hundreds of years."

"And how did you know that, Mr. Knowall?" demanded Wendy.

"There are some things that boys know naturally," said Pete loftily.

"Phooey!" exclaimed his sisters as one.

"It's true," put in Harry. "The sandstone was used every Sunday on the big sailing ships, and so it came to be known as holy."

Now the girls surveyed Harry closely.

"How interesting," said Pauline. "And how would a Missouri farm boy know such a thing?"

"I overheard your dad telling Pete yesterday."

"Ah, ha!" exclaimed the girls. "Clever Pete!"

# Chapter Ten

## *TREASURE ISLAND.*

Working with a will, the youngsters soon had the *Seawolf* looking her usual smart self. Then they trooped down below to find Mrs. Pallant finishing cleaning up as her husband penciled in the final courses on the charts.

"There we are," he announced. "These will be the new courses to steer."

The others gathered around as he explained: "We'll leave here and steer the course of 150 degrees for about a couple of hours until we are well clear of Sambro Island. Then a turn to the right on to 260 degrees will put us on a course for Pearl Island at the entrance to Mahone Bay. One more change to 320 should take us direct to Oak Island. I say 'should' because the bay is full of small islands and we will have to keep a sharp lookout to identify it."

"Let's go!" cried Pauline and soon they had cast off and were chugging slowly towards the great bridge. Everybody was on deck enjoying the fresh breeze, especially Pip, who soon took up his favorite job of acting figurehead.

"Hoist the sails!" shouted the skipper, obviously glad to be under way again. "With a breeze like this, we'll make good time."

Working like a professional team, the four quickly had every sail up and properly trimmed. The *Seawolf* immediately responded by heeling over to her favorite sailing angle. Traffic was lighter today and nothing hindered their smooth passage.

By the time lunch was over, they were out in deep water and running free with a long swell helping them along. With the boom swung well out and the boat riding steady, there was little to do except steer. The skipper was at the wheel and the mate comfortably seated in the cockpit with Pip, while the four sprawled in their favorite positions on the cabin roof.

Mrs. Pallant breathed deeply and exclaimed, "How peaceful this is!"

Pauline opened her eyes lazily and saw that Harry was studying her face closely. Then he turned slightly and did the same with her sister. "Something wrong, Harry?" she queried.

"Oh, no. I was just thinking how much your eyelashes are like a camel's. Wendy's are too."

"Harry!" both girls sat up, as though unable to believe their ears.

"Ho, ho, ho!" Pete exploded in a raucous hoot. "Harry is just trying to tell you that you both look like a couple of camels!"

"Oh, no!" Harry was horrified at the very idea. "I was just thinking that your eyelashes are as beautiful as a camel's."

"Oh?" said the girls together, with a frosty look at their cousin. Harry floundered on: "Didn't you know that camels have the most beautiful eyelashes?"

"Is that so?" asked Wendy, still in some doubt.

"I suppose that you are now going to tell us that you raise camels on the farm in Missouri," said Pauline.

"No, no!" Harry was wishing he had never started this thing. "I met a man on the plane who has adventured all over the world and he told me that camels have the most luxurious eyelashes, long and thick to guard against the glare of the desert sun and also to keep the sand out of their eyes during sandstorms."

"You girls don't recognise a compliment when you hear one," put in their mother. "You know that your father and I were in the Middle East for a few years, before you were born. There are lots of camels out there and I often used to admire their beautiful eyelashes, although it never occurred to me to wonder why they were like that. Incidentally, now that I come to think of it, nobody ever told me my eyelashes are as beautiful as those of a camel!"

"Ah, yes!" said her husband, getting the message. "I guess that proves we are all not as smart as Harry!"

Harry went on to tell them all a little about the exploits of Frank Shaw, and they listened closely.

"He sounds like a real old-timer," remarked the skipper. "You were lucky to meet him. He is the kind I enjoy talking to. That is one of the best things about travel: you get to meet the most interesting people, often in very unlikely places."

"By the way," put in his mate. "To return to the ordinary. I notice a very strange thing has happened on this ship." Having gained everyone's attention, she continued, "I have, somehow, become the cook, without even trying. I hope you noticed that lunch was served by somebody. Well, that was me! Supper can be prepared by volunteers."

"I don't mind volunteering," offered Harry.

"Good lad!" said the skipper from behind the wheel. "Pauline can be the other volunteer. And if she dishes up anymore sea soup, she'll be keelhauled!"

"I was just resting," sighed Pauline. "But I'll do my duty."

Pearl Island came into sight in the late afternoon and they soon had to change course. The *Seawolf* heeled over on the starboard tack without losing any speed. "Now," said the skipper, "Two hands to cooking, and the other two on lookout, one on each bow. Watch out for shoal water on any floating objects."

When supper was ready, they took turns to eat, while wheel and lookouts were kept manned. Islands soon began to appear on both sides, but only slight deviations from their course were required. After supper, it was all hands on deck again to watch for Oak Island.

Harry was the first to spot it, although he wasn't sure.

"That's it alright," agreed his uncle after careful study with the binoculars. "Exactly where it is supposed to be!"

"Treasure Island at last!" cried Wendy gleefully.

It looks the same as all the other islands to me," observed her mother.

"Where are we going to anchor, Dad?" asked Pete.

"We'll have to go around the other side of the island and try to find a sheltered spot."

But the skipper's plan did not work out. As they drew near the island, the wind veered sharply. This soon produced a broken cross sea, which made the *Seawolf* begin rolling heavily, losing half her speed. He studied the sea and sky carefully.

"I don't like this at all," he announced. "If this wind is going to hold, and it probably will, the sea will become even rougher on the other side of the island. I think we had better try to find some sort of shelter at the end, until the weather settles down."

"There's a boat coming around the far end of the island," announced Harry suddenly. Everybody turned to see a long, black motor boat speeding towards them.

"What kind is it?" asked Pete.

His father studied the craft through his binoculars. "She looks like a navy torpedo boat, although I don't see any guns or torpedo tubes. She is painted black overall and has no name on her bows. Nor is she flying any kind of an ensign. Curious to say the least."

"Maybe it's a modern pirate!" suggested Pauline.

"Or a smuggler," offered Wendy.

The skipper chuckled. "More likely a special delivery freight boat."

"It's coming awfully close," observed the mate.

The rakish looking craft was approaching at high speed, but suddenly it stopped its engines not far from the *Seawolf*. As it drifted slowly by, lifting and rolling violently, a side window of the enclosed wheelhouse slid open and a man with a megaphone stuck his head out. "Where are you bound?" he roared.

"None of your business," mustered the skipper to himself. Then, in a loud voice, he answered more politely: "Just a holiday cruise."

"Well, keep away from Oak Island, it's private property!"

The speaker pulled in his head abruptly and closed the window while the big speedboat shot forward, apparently continuing on a course around the island.

"What nerve!" exclaimed Mrs. Pallant. "Such hospitality!"

"What are you going to do, Dad?" asked Wendy.

"Carry on as planned. We don't intend anybody any harm, and in any case, no one should refuse shelter to a boat in bad weather. Fetch me my chart, please."

After studying the chart carefully, he announced: "There is a tiny bay at the very end of the island which just might be big enough to give us a safe anchorage. Everybody watch for the opening, and when we sight it, we'll drop the sails and take her in on the motor."

"I guess that boat was pretty fast," observed Harry. "It was soon out of sight."

"I know the type well," said his uncle. "They are seventy feet long and have three converted aircraft engines which give them a speed in excess of fifty knots. They are occasionally sold as surplus by the navy, and some buyers fit them with two ordinary motors because the original three have such a fantastic fuel consumption. But, judging by the way the boat shot away from here, I imagine she still has her original motors."

"I wonder who owns it?" put in his mate.

"I wonder too. It should at least have a name and show a registration number. I suppose it could belong to the owner of Oak Island, or even to those engineers who are supposed to be bringing out the treasure. It is quite likely that they have been pestered by people so much that they are determined to keep everybody away, at least during this critical time."

As he finished speaking, the skipper noticed a slight break in the trees near the water's edge and quickly focused his glasses on it. "Down sails," he ordered. "I think we have found our haven."

While the four were busy with the sheets and halyards, he started the motor and steered close to the shore. Suddenly robbed of the steadying influence of the wind on her sails, the *Seawolf* rolled even more heavily, and Pip would have slid overboard if Wendy had not grabbed his collar in the nick of time.

"Hang on everybody," shouted her father. "This won't last long."

A narrow entrance almost obscured by foliage was now discernible about a hundred yards ahead. As they wallowed towards it, the skipper instructed Pete to take the long boathook forward and went along to help, but fortunately, the water proved to be just deep enough for the schooner to enter.

It was a tricky business steering through the entrance because the masts could easily catch against the overhanging trees. The gap was not much wider than the boat first, then it suddenly widened into a tiny lagoon. There were scarcely enough room to turn the boat around so the engine had to be reversed quickly to avoid running aground.

There was little daylight left among the foliage, so no time was lost in getting four stout mooring lines ashore with the aid of the inflatable dinghy. The boys secured them to trees and returned on board just as darkness fell.

"Well done, boys," said the skipper. "Now, I hope we can relax for the night."

With the boat on an even keel again, the mate was able to prepare an excellent supper which all could enjoy at a steady table.

"This is weird," observed Harry. "Like being moved suddenly from the open sea into the middle of a forest! It seems odd to be on a boat with trees pressing all around."

"It will seem spooky later on!" said Pauline mischievously.

"How long will we be staying here, Dad?" asked Wendy.

"If the weather is reasonable tomorrow, we'll sail around the island and then carry on back to Halifax. If it isn't, I guess we'll have to stay here until it is."

"If we have to stay, can we go ashore?" asked Wendy eagerly.

"We'll see. The thing to do now is get a good night's sleep. Believe me, I need it."

An hour later, the *Seawolf* was in darkness, riding comfortably in the middle of the hidden lagoon.

*Bertram Smith*

# Chapter Eleven

## *THE HIDDEN CAVE.*

Next morning, everybody slept late. The skipper was awake first, but as he dressed, the boys stirred too and they were on deck not long after him. The wind had died away completely and it was a beautiful day with the sun already high in a clear sky, although only patches of it were visible through the trees.

"Gosh! This lagoon is tiny," exclaimed Harry. "We can almost jump ashore. It didn't seem so small last night."

"It wasn't," replied his uncle who was sitting comfortably on the cabin roof smoking his pipe and studying a book of tide tables. "When we came in the tide was higher. Now it is low—just beginning to flood the fact."

"How can you tell?" asked the boy, obviously interested.

"It's easy enough in a place like this. If you watch the entrance and you'll see the current flowing in. Keep your eye on that small piece of driftwood coming in now."

The two boys looked towards the narrow entrance and saw a splinter of wood moving slowly but steadily into the enclosed area. Making themselves comfortable, they watched it drift towards the boat. Just short of the bows it changed direction and headed towards a clump of bushes overhanging the bank on the other side.

Pete puzzled over this for a moment. "How? Well, I suppose it stays in here until the tide changes and then goes out the way it came in. Why?"

"Because that piece of wood has drifted out of sight under those bushes and there seems to be quite a current flowing. Where could it be going?" Mr. Pallant stared at the bushes and saw several twigs and leaves drift along and disappear under them. "That's interesting. Maybe there's a small stream hidden among those bushes."

"Can we take the dinghy and investigate?" asked Pete eagerly.

"If you think it's worthwhile. It will be an hour or two before we can get underway, but I don't suppose breakfast will be too long, so don't go wandering around the island."

"O.K. Dad. Come on, Harry. Let's do some exploring!"

He could not have asked for a more willing helper, and a few minutes later they were approaching the bushes.

"I'll paddle from the stern now," said Pete. "You get in the bows and see if you can find an opening."

Harry did so and soon announced that he had found one. "It looks like a little stream. Just wide enough for us to get through." Taking hold of the branches on each side, he pulled the dinghy forward.

After a few feet of dense, overhanging branches, the stream widened a little and they were able to sit up and take stock of their surroundings. Branches were thoroughly intertwined above their heads so that they were in a cool green tunnel about three feet high, shot through with shafts of sunlight, where the sun was able to penetrate the thick foliage. It was a quiet, eerie place and the boys subconsciously spoke in whispers.

"This is a weird place," said Pete. "What do you think, Harry?"

"Kind of greeny-gloomy," grinned the other. It's only an overgrown stream. Let's see what is around that bend."

A few feet ahead, the narrow stream curved out of sight. Pete pushed an oar against some branches to make the boat move forward and soon Harry was peering around the bend. "Take it easy, Pete," he whispered. "There's a cave, or a tunnel ahead, I think."

Pete could hardly wait for the boat to move far enough ahead for him to be able to see that the stream disappeared into an opening in a rock face. Evidently, there was a small hill or cliff hidden among the trees. The opening was not much larger than the dinghy, and water bubbled and gurgled as it flowed steadily in.

"I wonder where it leads to," said Pete, as they held the boat steady at the entrance and peered cautiously inside. It could have been either a cave or a tunnel, but the interior was so dark they were unable to tell.

"Let's go inside," suggested Pete.

But his cousin was more doubtful. "I don't think we should go in without a flashlight. And we should let your dad know, too."

"There can't be any harm in just looking inside."

Harry suddenly had a vision of a tiny boat shooting over the edge of a subterranean waterfall and disappearing into the bowels of the Earth. "Suppose there's a waterfall or some rapids inside?"

Pete thought for a moment. "Listen!" he said suddenly.

Harry held his breath and strained his ears.

"Hear anything?" asked Pete.

"No."

"That proves it's safe then. Rapids or a waterfall would make a noise, especially in an enclosed space, and we would be able to hear it even outside."

Harry looked at his cousin admiringly. "Good thinking!" All right, let's just peep inside."

Carefully, they edged the boat forward by pulling on the rocky sides, but inside it widened suddenly, and at the same time, the roof rose out of their reach. Now they were drifting with the current into complete darkness.

Looking back, they could see the green glow of daylight at the entrance, but it was not strong enough to penetrate into this dark and gloomy place. In fact, the patch of light was beginning to seem like a very fragile link with the outside world.

Neither of the boys were feeling very brave now, and almost together they suddenly remarked, "Maybe we should turn back now!"

Groping around for the oars, Pete fumbled as he tried to fit them into the rowlocks. "Hurry up!" hissed his cousin. "I can hear water rushing!"

Sure enough, the gentle gurgle had become louder, and the sound now beginning to echo from the rocky walls. At last, Pete managed to get the oars working and began to pull hard to stop the boat drifting and make it move against the current. Slowly the dim entrance drew near and they both began to breathe easier. After what seemed a long time, they were close enough to be able to ship oars and grasp the rocky sides.

"Wow!" gasped Pete as they shot into the green gloom outside. "That was beginning to get exciting!"

"It sure was! That's the last time I'll go into a dark, spooky place without a flashlight!"

"I wouldn't mind going back there with one, though," said Pete.

"I'm willing," Harry assured his cousin. "Maybe we can persuade Uncle to come too."

"I don't think he will need much persuading," grinned Pete. "When they hear about it, the whole family will want to come!"

Back at the schooner, everybody was on deck awaiting their return. They had been away longer than they had realised and breakfast was ready. The girls in particular were very curious to know where they had been, and between mouthfuls the boys made their little adventure sound as thrilling as possible.

The skipper looked very interested. "I would like to see that. I'll take a flashlight and have a look directly after breakfast."

"Not alone, you won't," said his wife firmly.

"I'll go!" exclaimed both girls simultaneously.

"It may be dangerous. I will go," insisted their mother.

"You can't go without us!" exclaimed Harry, obviously horrorstruck at the very idea.

"Of course not," seconded Pete. "After all, we found it."

His father laughed. "Rally an adventurous crew! I suppose if Pip could talk, he would have a good reason for going, too. However, he can't, we'll leave him to guard the boat while the rest of us go."

For once, there was no lack of help clearing up after a meal, and soon they were stepping into the unsteady dinghy which was barely big enough to hold them all. Pip stood on the deck watching them questioningly with his head titled to one side.

"Can't he come too?" asked Wendy, who could never resist an appealing look.

"There isn't room," said her father. "Anyhow, I very much doubt he would enjoy exploring a dark cave. Stay there, Pip, Stay!"

The dog sat down obediently, but he watched longingly as they pulled across the small lagoon. Within minutes, they were working carefully into the green passage leading to the cave. The girls were thrilled at the way it opened up and yet remained so well hidden.

"Maybe nobody in the whole entire world knows about this," whispered Pauline in awe.

"That is possible," agreed her father. "So there is no need to whisper. I don't suppose anybody is listening!"

"There is the entrance!" exclaimed Mrs. Pallant. "It looks too small for this boat to go through."

But the dinghy went through without difficulty as everybody held on to the rock walls and guided it carefully. Pete shone his flashlight from the bows, and after a little more than a boat's length, the tunnel suddenly became higher and wider. As they drifted forward with the current, the probing beam showed walls and roof of black rock.

"This is creepy," said Wendy in hushed tones. "I wonder where it leads to?"

"We should know pretty soon," said her father. "Listen and we should hear that sound of rushing water that the boys mentioned."

Everybody listened intently and soon they could hear the gurgling and bubbling of water entering a confined space.

"Keep the light up ahead, Pete," instructed the skipper. "I will hold the oars ready, in case we have to stop quickly."

As he was speaking, the boat was moving forward through the darkness in the track of a flashlight which told them no more than they were in a flooded cave.

"Hold it!" cried Pete suddenly. "We are coming to a dead end!"

His light now revealed a solid rock wall ahead. Mr. Pallant used his oars to slow the boat down. The sound of rushing water was now very loud, and Pete quickly found the reason. His light revealed a hole low down in the wall through which the water was pouring and gushing. It was similar to the entrance except that it was only inches in height instead of feet.

Letting the boat drift gently against the rock face, the skipper used his own flashlight to examine the cave. "Well," he said a little later, "It looks as though we are in a long cave with a stream running through it into an underground tunnel. Obviously we can't go any further, so we may as well go back. I'll turn the boat around."

As the dinghy approached the dimly lit entrance, Pete casually swung the beam of his flashlight around to make sure nothing had been overlooked. Mr. Pallant was busy rowing, with his back towards the bow, so it was Harry who first saw their danger.

"Look!" he exclaimed. "The entrance is nearly closed!"

All eyes swung together to see that the entrance was much smaller than when they had entered. The skipper began rowing as hard as he could.

"The tide has risen much quicker than expected," he said. "Heads down everybody, and push against the walls as we go through. We might just do it."

After a couple of extra strong strokes, he pulled the oars inboard and crouched low. The current was now running strongly against them and everybody had to push extra hard against the walls to make the boat move forward. It was touch and go, and they all had to practically lie down in the boat as both sides scraped the rough rock, but they managed to work through it.

"Whew! We only just made it," said the skipper as they cleared the opening and were able to sit up again. "That—what's the matter, Wendy?"

The girl was almost bursting with excitement and practically speechless, "Did you seem them, Dad?" she finally managed to squeak. "Did you see them?"

All the others were holding onto the branches to keep the boat stationary and they stared at her in surprise.

"Did I see what?" demanded her father.

"Just inside the entrance, to the right, in the corner," bubbled Wendy. "I saw them just as Pete put his flashlight out to duck down in the boat."

"Well, what did you see?" demanded Pauline. "Dragons or something?"

"Steps!" declared her sister, her eyes glowing. "Steps cut in the rock and leading to a dark opening. And a rusty old ringbolt fixed to the wall for tying up boats!"

There was dead silence in the boat, broken only by the gurgle of water hurrying into the cave.

"Are you sure?" asked the skipper at last.

"Positive, Dad, I saw the steps clearly."

There was another brief silence until Harry asked: "Uncle, do you remember in the story you told us about the Oak Island treasure, somebody put some dye in the treasure pit and colored water came out on the far side of the island. Do you think this might be where it came from?"

"I was wondering the same thing. I don't remember reading about anybody finding exactly where the colored water actually came from. This could well be the place."

"It sure is well hidden," said Pauline excitedly. "Maybe we really have found a back-door to the treasure!"

"Maybe," agreed her father with a smile. "I guess we'll have to go in there again and do a little exploring."

But her mother was not so sure. "It seems pretty dangerous to me. Maybe we had better mind our own business."

"Oh Mom!" there was a chorus of protest.

"Well, suppose we had been trapped down there?" she persisted.

"We would have had to wait around until the tide went down again," said the skipper reassuringly. "Next time, we'll go in when the tide is falling and then we will have several hours available."

"When will that be?" asked Harry eagerly.

"Well, it will be high tide in about a couple of hours, so the water will be back down to this level in about four hours. It is now lunch time, so I think we might try again just after supper. And now back to the *Seawolf*."

Pip welcomed them as though they had been away for a month, and after calming him down, everybody helped to prepare the meal.

"So many willing helpers all of a sudden!" declared the mate. "You must all be very hungry."

"Not me," said Pete. "I'm too excited to eat." But when they sat down, he somehow managed to eat enough for two as usual, even though breakfast had been late.

"What if we find the treasure?" wondered Wendy. "Will it belong to us?"

"I'm afraid not," her father said. "Although I expect that we would be able to claim a share of it. But let's not count our chickens too soon. Those steps might not lead anywhere in particular."

Harry's face fell. "Do you really think so?"

"No, I don't think anything. I'm trying to keep an open mind. We'll soon find out though!"

*Bertram Smith*

# Chapter Twelve

## TRAPPED!

There was a tiny beach on one side of the lagoon, and the next few hours were spent sun-bathing and swimming. But, pleasant though it was, the four youngsters were eager for time to pass. They could think of nothing else but those stone steps leading up into that dark cavern.

As Pauline insisted: "That has to be passage to the treasure chamber. What else could it be?" The others could not even think of an answer.

At last it was suppertime, and never was a meal more welcome, although none of the four felt particularly hungry. They would have bolted their food quickly down the hatch had not Mrs. Pallant kept a watchful eye on them.

"Take your time and eat plenty, or you may be hungry before we get back," she warned.

"Who wants to waste time eating when we could be searching for pirate loot?" grumbled Pete. "Why can't we go now?"

"Those who don't eat don't go," declared his father, and there was no more argument.

As the meal drew to a close, the skipper said, "We'll take every flashlight we have and also some matches. Wendy, you put them all in the old leather bag and they will be easier to carry."

A sad-eyed Pip watched them all climb carefully into the dinghy and leave him alone again. "Never mind Pip," called Wendy. "We won't be long, and then you'll be wearing a diamond studded collar!"

Willing hands quickly pulled the boat through the bushes and trees to the tunnel entrance. Now the tide was low enough to expose more of it, and the dinghy slid through easily. Wendy passed out a flashlight each and, immediately once they were inside, all six beams focused in the corner on the right. Sure enough, narrow stone steps, glistening wet, lead up to an opening several feet above the water level.

"Just as Wendy described!" exclaimed the skipper. "Those steps are obviously man-made, and as there is no sign of wear, they can't have been used very much."

"And there's the ringbolt," declared Pete, turning his light on to a large ringbolt set deep into the stone.

"H'm! Very old and very rusty, but still strong enough for the job. Tie the boat up to it, Pete, and then I will investigate that opening up there," instructed his father.

"Can I come?" asked Pauline in a voice trembling with excitement.

"Me too!" said Pete. As he made a quick hitch on the ring.

"Nobody is coming," declared their father. "At least not until I have a look. I won't be long."

"Be careful, dear," Mrs. Pallant warned her husband as he gingerly climbed the slippery steps. A minute later, he was standing at the top, directing his light through the opening. Then he disappeared, only to reappear almost immediately.

His voice echoed eerily around the cavern as he announced: "There's a tunnel up here, dry and high enough to walk along. Come on everybody, and use your lights on the steps because they are very slippery." Then, as though forgetting his own warning, he added quickly, "Hurry!" There was a boyish excitement in his voice and it was obvious that he could hardly wait for them.

When they were all assembled at the tunnel entrance, he led the way cautiously along the rocky tunnel. After a few yards, it curved to the left and then straightened out.

"Single file," ordered the skipper. "I'll take the lead. Who wants to act as rear guard?"

There was a short silence and then his wife said, "I will. Then I can be sure of being first out if we are suddenly attacked by pirates!"

"Good girl! Use your light and I'll use mine. The others can save theirs for the future."

They proceeded slowly, stumbling occasionally on the uneven floor which was thick with dust. Swinging his light steadily from side to side, the skipper suddenly caught a glint of steel from the corner of his eye. Whirling rapidly, he tensed for action. Then he exploded into laughter. His light had revealed the four, crouched in line ahead, each with a drawn sheath-knife held at the ready. And, judging by their fierce expressions, prepared to fight to the death!

It was this display of steel that had reflected his light, and finding themselves suddenly the center of attention, the youngsters joined in the laughter.

"We were ready for anything!" grinned Pauline as they all returned their knives to their belts.

"I don't blame them for being prepared," put in her mother. "I keep thinking someone is going to jump on me from behind!"

"All right," acknowledged the skipper. "You two boys can bring up the rear. I suppose, if you want to, you could walk abreast."

The boys quickly took up the rear position and, without discussing it, they did so side by side. The party set off again along the dark tunnel, and subconsciously, the hands of the four strayed to their knife handles.

A few minutes later the leader's light picked out a small, square object lying to one side and thickly covered in dust. Coming to a stop, they all peered at it as every flashlight came into play.

"What is it?" whispered Harry.

His uncle chuckled. "I don't suppose anybody has been along this way for at least a hundred years, so there is no need to whisper!" As he spoke, he was nudging the duty object with his foot. "By thunder, it's an old-fashioned ship's lantern. Broken, which is probably why it was left behind, but it proves that some sailormen have been through here, even if it was a long time ago."

Moments later, he halted again with his light shining down in front of him. It showed a flat stone slab, several feet in length forming part of the tunnel floor. "Now, what would this be for?" he wondered as the others crowded around him.

"This is the treasure pit!" declared Harry with conviction.

"Well, the stone was put there for some special reason, I imagine, and judging by the thickness of the dust on it, nobody has walked over it in a very long, long time."

"It's thick all right," agreed Harry, as he scraped the toe of his shoe across the slab.

"Look! There's some writing on the stone," squeaked Wendy excitedly. Bending down, she brushed her hand over the mark left by Harry's shoe. All lights immediately focused on that spot, and sure enough, some faint lettering could be seen where the lettering had been disturbed.

"Now is the time to use those knives," said her father quickly. "Dig out those letters!"

Four knives flashed together, regardless of dusty knees, the owners went to work with a will.

"Here we are," announced Pete as he cleared some words. "It says 'this stone'."

"Some help!" snorted Pauline. "We know it's a stone. There must be some more letters."

The surface of the stone was far from smooth, and the old-fashioned lettering had apparently been cut in by an amateur using a blunt tool, so it is not easy to decipher. Harry scratched away impatiently, eager to be the first to read the message.

"Got it!" he exclaimed triumphantly. "It says, *'Beneath this stone fabulous treasure lies'.*"

"I told you! I told you!" cried Pete. "This is it!"

"That's not right," declared Pauline, peering over her cousin's shoulder. "The letters don't fit." Leaning across, she scraped some more. "I thought so. The first word is 'beyond' not 'beneath'."

"There is some more down here," said Wendy, industriously scraping lower down. "If only some people would make room."

It did not take long to uncover the rest of the message and they all read it in silence:

### *BEYOND THIS STONE*

### *FABULOUS TREASURE*

### *LIES WELL GUARDED*

### *PROCEED AT YOUR PERIL*

Mrs. Pallant was the first to speak. "I think we should go back. They can keep their old treasure."

"The warning is clear enough," admitted her husband. "Although, I wonder if the peril still exists after nearly two hundred years?"

"Let's just go on a little way," suggested Pauline.

"Yes, let's," chorused the other three.

Mr. Pallant shone his light along the tunnel. The beam was just long enough to show a bend up ahead. "I'll tell you what we'll do," he said. "You all stay here for a couple of minutes while I go as far as that bend is in the tunnel. I want to find out if there is anything in sight."

Without waiting for further comment, he set off over the stone slab. But before he could reach the far end, he staggered and gave a startled cry. The slab was sinking beneath his weight. With a creaking groan, it was tilting, and the end nearest the others was rising amidst a shower of dust. From below came the sound of rushing water.

For one frightening moment, the others were all paralyzed with shock, then, acting as one, the two boys flung themselves on the still-rising end of the huge stone. Their combined weight stopped it tilting just as the skipper was losing his footing. Now he was able to grasp the sides of the hole and haul himself to safety.

Slowly and creakingly, the mantrap returned to its original position, but not before Pete was able to shine his light into the blackness below. It was reflected by swiftly flowing water, hissing and gurgling in the narrow space. Then both sight and sound were cut off as the stone levelled itself with a dull thud.

"Diabolical!" exclaimed the skipper as he scrambled to his feet. His wife edged carefully past the edge of the stone slab, anxious to make sure he was unhurt. The others followed somberly.

"That was a close shave," he continued as he brushed dust from his clothes. "Fortunately, the trap worked sluggishly. It was probably perfectly balanced when it was installed, but rust and dirt in the mechanisms slowed it down. Even so, I would have fallen in if not for the quick thinking of Pete and Harry. Thank you, boys, well done!" he added, turning his light on them, "I don't know whether you saved my life or not, but it seems mighty like it!"

"You boys were so brave! And what was that water down there?" asked Wendy with a shudder.

"That must be the underground stream we saw rushing into the underground tunnel," replied her father. "It seems very likely that it is also the water which guards the treasure."

"Now perhaps you'll go back?" wondered Mrs. Pallant.

Her husband laughed ruefully. "As usual, I should have listened to you, my dear. I guess we had better go back. Come on, everybody."

There was a combined groan from the two boys who were both feeling adventurous.

"Listen!" exclaimed Wendy. "Footsteps!"

Everybody froze as they heard the muffled but unmistakable sound of footsteps approaching from the direction in which they had been heading.

Spines tingling, they swung their flashlights simultaneously, the beams stabbing the blackness like miniature searchlights. After a little wavering, the beams settled on the walker. It was Pauline, strolling along as casually as though she were returning from a shopping trip. She blinked surprised when she found herself the center of so much attention.

"Pauline!" exclaimed her mother after a moment of stunned silence. "Where have you been?"

They were all dumbfounded to find that Pauline had slipped away. In fact, Wendy had been so sure that her sister was behind her that she glanced quickly over her shoulder, just in case there was another one!

"What on earth are you doing, wandering about in the dark?" demanded the skipper.

"When I knew you were safe, I decided to stroll along and have a look around that bend to save you the trouble," replied Pauline innocently. "I used my light going, but I suppose nobody noticed it in all the excitement. Coming back, I didn't need it because, looking from the other direction, your lights brighten the whole tunnel."

"Well, you gave us an awful shock," said her mother severely. "I hope none of you wander off again."

"We thought you were a pirate!" chuckled Pete.

Then the skipper remembered. "Well, did you see anything beyond that bend?"

Pauline paused deliberately before she admitted, "Yes, I did!"

There was a short silence which was finally broken by her exasperated sister. "Well, what are you waiting for?"

"I just wanted to be sure you were all listening!" replied Pauline sweetly. "I saw a door in the distance and it was wide open."

"What kind of door?" asked her father.

"A wooden one. At least the barrier is of wood, so I suppose the door would be the same although I couldn't see it."

"You mean it opens the other way?"

"I suppose so," she answered.

"Let's go have a look!" suggested Harry.

"If we don't, we'll probably spend the rest of our lives wondering about it!" grinned Wendy.

"That's right!" exclaimed Pete.

"You have a point there, Wendy," agreed her father. "I don't suppose there could be any harm in looking through the doorway!"

After a moment's silence, Mrs. Pallant said, "You are as bad as they are. I suppose I would never hear the end of it if I insisted on turning back now. Let's go, but be very careful."

Amid a chorus of chuckles they moved forward again, but this time with every flashlight in full play. So far, the tunnel had maintained a fairly constant width about six feet and a little more than that in height, but as they followed the curve, the width more than doubled, and there was a corresponding increase in height.

Soon they were all standing in front of a wooden barrier extending the full width and height of the tunnel, but with a wide doorway in the center. The skipper examined the barrier curiously. "This is built of old's ship's timbers, he announced. "Good and strong and jammed tight against the walls and ceiling."

"They forgot to fit the door," said Pete as he peered through the opening.

"Apparently so," agreed his father. "The posts are grooved to take a door, but maybe it was never delivered."

"A good thing it wasn't," commented Mrs. Pallant. "It was probably intended to be a trap of some kind."

"That could be, so maybe it's one we missed."

"But why would they want a door here?" asked Wendy. "There doesn't seem to be anything on the other side."

All the flashlights were trained through the doorway but, apart from the fact that the tunnel reduced to its original size a little farther along, it was apparently exactly the same beyond the barrier.

Cautiously, they all passed through the doorway and the skipper shone his light on the other side of the wooden barricade. "Just the same on this side—" he was beginning to say when he caught sight of something glinting above his head.

"Hello, what's this?" he demanded, shining his light upwards.

Everybody stopped to stare.

"It's a cutlass!" exclaimed Pete. "A real pirate cutlass. Gee, what a find!"

The point of the blade of a heavy cutlass had been pushed several inches into a knothole in the heavy planking above the doorway, so that the weapon was sticking almost straight out.

"That's an odd place to leave it," commented the skipper. Taking a grip on the dusty handle he gave it a sharp tug. But the weapon did not move. "Stand clear, everybody. I want to give it a good strong pull."

Exerting all of his strength and weight, he gave a mighty heave and the cutlass left its hole suddenly, causing him to fall over backwards.

"Lookout!" yelled Harry as there came a rumble from above, followed by a rattling crash which shook the very rock under their feet. A cloud of dust obscured the view a moment, and then they were able to see that a massive wooden door now fitted snugly in the doorway.

There was dead silence. On his feet again, the skipper carefully examined the door. "It must weigh nearly a ton," he said huskily.

"What happened?" asked Pete.

"We've sprung the second trap," replied his father. "The door was there all the time, but we just didn't think of it dropping down through a pocket door slot from the ceiling. Of course, the cutlass was acting as a locking bar and supporting it."

"But why go to so much trouble?" asked Mrs. Pallant. "Why not fit an ordinary door and lock it?"

Her husband shook his head. "Anybody who survived that first trap would not be stopped by an ordinary door."

There was silence again as they stared with sinking hearts at the formidable barrier which now cut them off from the outside world.

## Chapter Thirteen

# THE DREAMER.

"The fiends!" The skipper spoke first. "The monster who figured all of this out knew that anybody who saw the cutlass in that position would not be able to resist trying to pull it out."

"He certainly didn't intend that person to get out," said his wife with a tremor in her voice.

The skipper was tight-lipped. "Yes, I suppose those men figured that if anybody was persistent enough to get this far, there was not much hope of being able to keep them out, so the best alternative was to keep them in. And we happen to be the first to walk into the trap. What a fool I've been," he added bitterly. "I should have known that men who went to so much trouble to safeguard the treasure at the money pit would not leave a back door open. This place is probably full of booby-traps. We are fighting men who have been dead nearly two hundred years, and I can almost hear them laughing at us."

Pauline suddenly began to sob. "It's all my fault!" she cried. "If I hadn't gone snooping around, we might all be safely back on our boat by now."

Both her parents moved over to put an arm around her shoulders. "It's not your fault at all," said her father. "I am the one responsible, so don't worry about that."

"What shall we do now?" asked Harry, who was feeling both scared and thrilled at the same time.

"Well," said his uncle. "We can't go back, and there's no use staying here, so we have to go forward."

"Do you think there could be another way out, Dad?" asked Pete.

"You never know." Mr. Pallant was trying to sound a lot more cheerful than he felt. "A lot has happened since this treasure was hidden away, and all kinds of changes may have taken place. When you think of the developments during the last few years alone, we might turn the next corner and find ourselves in a new subway. Then we would have to watch out for trains!" His humor sounded a little forced. "Come on, follow me carefully, and save your flashlights as much as possible."

The tunnel continued in a fairly straight line for what seemed a long distance, and even the skipper hesitated to estimate how far they had traveled since leaving the *Seawolf*. Without thinking, Harry yawned loudly, and immediately all of the others began yawing too. His aunt turned her wristwatch towards the nearest flashlight.

"Ten-thirty! We've been in here longer than I thought, You children must be tired. I know I am. We really must stop for a rest."

"This is only a small island," said Pete. "So the tunnel can't go on much longer. Let's keep going for a few minutes."

"That's true," agreed his father. "It must lead somewhere soon."

They continued their cautious journey, but by this time, the skipper's flashlight was growing weak and showed only a few feet ahead. Suddenly, he gave an exclamation and stopped dead. The others crowded around and switched on their lights. Facing them was a blank wall of rock. They had reached the end of the tunnel.

"This can't be the end, surely," said Wendy. "We must have missed a turn or a branch or something."

"Maybe," her father did not sound very convinced. "Look around everybody, and make sure."

Five minutes later, a careful search had revealed nothing, and he gave the order to conserve the flashlights. "It's a dead end all right. Take a rest, everybody. I'm afraid we shall have to spend the night here after all."

Silently, they all made themselves as comfortable as possible, sitting with their backs against the rough stone walls. Pete was using his flashlight to examine the walls and ceiling. "Dad, do you think this tunnel is natural, or did somebody dig it out?"

"I was wondering that myself, and I've been watching carefully as we came along. There are definite signs of metal tools being used here and there, but I would guess the tunnel is mainly natural. Somebody widened it where necessary to make it usable."

"But surely neither man nor nature would make a dead-end tunnel," put in Mrs. Pallant.

"It doesn't seem very likely," agreed her husband. "I think a natural tunnel would be more likely to reduce gradually in the form of a crack in the rock. Maybe that's what happened here and the men who built that door went to the trouble of widening it."

"But why stop suddenly?" asked Harry.

"That is the question. Either they gave up the job before it was finished, which seems hardly likely after coming so far, or there is a way out which we haven't found. Anyhow, I think the best thing we can do now is rest. We are all tired, and we should be able to tackle the problem better after some sleep."

There was much shuffling and wriggling as they all tried to make themselves comfortable on the stony ground and then all of the lights were turned off. The blackness was intense.

A few moments later Mrs. Pallant sighed and remarked, "I feel awfully hemmed in."

"I feel awfully hungry," said Pauline.

"I was waiting for somebody to say that," chuckled Wendy in the darkness. "I think I'll have a snack!"

Five flashlights snapped on and held her in focus.

"What do you mean?" It sounded as though everybody spoke at once.

She was holding the leather bag across her knees, and there was a wide grin on her face as she pulled out a packet of cookies and some bars of chocolate.

"Bless your heart, Wendy!" exclaimed her mother.

"We'll never tease you again about always eating!" promised her father jovially. "You've caught us this time."

"I thought a snack might come in handy," said Wendy. "There was plenty of room in the bag and I never know when I'm going to feel hungry." She passed the food around, and soon everybody's spirits began to rise as they munched happily with the aid of a single flashlight.

"Yes, it's true: even Wendy can be useful," commented Pete mischievously.

"Any more from you—" began Wendy, but she was interrupted by an exclamation from Harry.

"Ugh! What was that? Something is dripping down my neck."

"Probably blood!" suggested Pauline helpfully.

"Pirate's blood, of course!" added Wendy.

"Oh, you girls!" cried their mother.

"Keep still, Harry." The skipper moved closer and focused his light on the back of the boy's neck. "It's water," he announced and then shone his light upward. A steady drip of water was emerging from a crack in the roof. Now, I wonder where that comes from. Move over, Harry." He examined the floor carefully. "This has happened often before. Water has dripped down and then run away through this crack in the angle between the floor and the wall."

He caught a few drops in one hand and tasted them. "It's fresh water; probably rainwater. Maybe it's raining outside."

"That means the crack in the roof leads to the surface," said Pete. "If we could widen it enough, we might be able to make our way out."

"It's worth thinking about," agreed his father. "I wish we had some tools, although whether it would be a matter of feet or yards to dig, we have no way of knowing."

"Can we drink that water?" asked Pauline. "I'm awfully thirsty."

"We can if we have something to catch it in." replied her father. "Has anyone got any kind of cup or tin?"

Wendy was shining her light inside the packet to collect the last cookie crumbs when she noticed the texture of the cardboard.

"Look!" she exclaimed. "This packet is made from waxed cardboard. Maybe it will hold the water."

"It should," her father took it from her and held it under the steady drip from the roof. It proved to be watertight and in a matter of minutes, they were all able to enjoy a cool drink.

"Both food and drink," remarked Harry with a sigh. "Things don't seem so bad now. Thank you, Wendy, you saved the day!"

"Yes, Wendy, well done!" everybody clapped her on the back, while her mother wrapped her arms around her in a warm, comforting hug.

"I'm very proud of you, Wendy, for being prepared for anything," her father beamed with pride of her ingenuity.

"Things will surely seem a lot better when we find a way out of here," sighed her mother.

"Don't worry, my dear. We'll get out somehow, I feel sure," put in the skipper reassuringly. He was examining the roof and walls as he spoke when his eye caught something. "Hello, what's this?"

The others all stared as his light picked out what looked like a stick protruding from the wall at an angle some five feet up.

"Don't touch it!" exclaimed his wife. "It may be another trap. If you pull it down the roof will fall or something."

"All right. I'm just looking," he said, examining the stick closely. "This end has been badly burned. I wonder—oh. I see what it is—or was."

"What is it, Dad?" asked Pauline as she moved closer.

"Some kind of torch used as a light when men were working here. That is why it is stuck into the wall at this angle. It finally burned out, of course."

Without thinking, he had lowered the ray of his light to the floor, and this time, Harry spotted something. "Somebody left a club behind," he said as he shone his light on a dust-covered, club-shaped object lying near the wall.

The skipper stooped to examine it. "By thunder! It's a spare torch, I do believe it."

He picked the object up and knocked it against the wall to shake off the thick dust. "Yes, it is a pitch-pine torch, all right. I wonder if it could be any good after all these years?"

Taking a cigarette lighter from his pocket, he applied the flame to a thick coat of pitch at one end of the wood. Nothing happened first, then it started to sputter and crackle as the pitch softened. Finally, it caught fire, and soon they had a fiery, smoky torch which threw weird shadows on the walls and roof.

Pulling the spent torch from the wall, he stuck the new one in the slot and stepped back. "Now we have light. Things are really improving!"

"Look!" exclaimed Pete. "The smoke is going up through the crack in the roof. That proves it goes all the way to the surface."

"You're right," his father agreed as they all watched the smoke being drawn steadily towards the crack. "There is definitely a current of air through there. We'll investigate it thoroughly when we've had some sleep."

They all settled down again in much better spirits.

"I just got used to sleeping on a rocking boat," quipped Wendy. "And now I have to start all over again with a rocky floor! Good thing there are some dents as well as bumps so I can fit my bony parts in them."

"Some of the dents are filled with soft powder or whatever it is," said Pauline. "I've found a big one here and it's quite comfortable. Incidentally, I always wanted to be on a treasure island, but I never thought of being inside one!"

"Don't you wish you had such brilliantly witty sisters, Harry?" yawned Pete.

But his cousin was not listening. Harry had moved to the opposite side of the tunnel, away from the dripping water, and had made himself reasonably comfortable, but something was bothering him. At first, he did not know what it was. Then he realised it was a faint noise. "Listen!" he said suddenly.

Everybody turned to stare at him and in the dead silence they all heard a faint sigh coming from somewhere close by.

"Did anybody do that?" demanded the skipper. "No tricks, now."

None of them had, and as they all listened again, the sigh was repeated, louder and more prolonged. They exchanged uneasy glances, while the smoky flames threw weird, jerky shadows all around.

Every spine tingled as the sound came again, like a sigh from another world.

Mr. Pallant got to his feet carefully and shone his light around. "There must be an explanation for that noise," he said.

"There had better be," put in his wife fervently.

"I can feel a faint breeze," said Wendy who was sitting nearest to where the water dripped from the roof. She put her hand over the crack between the wall and the floor where the water was seeping away. "Yes, here it is. Air is coming up through this crack."

Her father put his hand over hers for a moment and nodded. "I think I have it. Air is forced up through this crack as the tide rises in the stream below. Air can't get out at the entrance because it is completely blocked with water, so it has to come out here. The crack is so small that the pressure probably builds up slightly and creates a sighing noise as it escapes." He gave a chuckle. "There is always a logical explanation if you look hard enough for it."

"I was sure it was a pirate sighing because he thought we were going to take his treasure!" said Pauline mischievously.

"Now, perhaps we can get some sleep," sighed her father as he sat down again.

But they were not to get very much sleep. About an hour later, Wendy began to twitch and then toss and turn restlessly. Abruptly, she stopped only to give a shriek which seemed to swell and gather volume in the confined space before reverberating and echoing away along the tunnel.

The others woke with a jolt and groped for their flashlights.

"What on earth was that?" demanded Pete.

"I think it was Wendy," whispered his mother, speaking from previous experience. All eyes swung in that direction and sure enough, Wendy was the only one still asleep.

"She must be having a bad dream," her mother explained. "She used to have them quite often, but they haven't bothered her much lately and I was hoping she was growing out of dreaming of such things. I suppose the experiences of the last few hours have brought one on, and no wonder. There is no need to worry. I will sit with her, comfort her. You all can go back to sleep."

But just as her mother finished speaking, Wendy gave a blood-curdling howl and sat up with her eyes wide open, although she was obviously still asleep.

"Phew!" murmured Pete as the howl fled along the echoing tunnel. "That was enough to make your spine curl!"

Wendy's big eyes stared unseeingly in front of her for a little longer until the soothing voice of her mother gradually penetrated her consciousness. Then she awoke with a start and began to sob. Mrs. Pallant had moved over and put her arms around Wendy's shoulders, giving her the warmest motherly hug. She knew well from experience that all would be well again soon. Slowly the cries died away.

"What was it, my darling? Did you have a bad dream?"

"I sure did," shuddered the girl. "And I'm glad it's over."

"What happened?" asked Pauline. She rarely dreamed herself and envied her sister such exciting dream exploits.

"We were all prisoners on a pirate ship," began Wendy softly. "It was a beautiful starlit night and we were all lying on deck with the big sails towering above us. The masts seemed very, very high and the rigging looked like gossamer webs spread across the stars. But there was nothing moving and the ship was absolutely quiet. It seemed awfully weird.

"Then the dawn came and soon the decks were filled with pirates. They wore old-fashioned clothes and had pistols and daggers stuck in their broad leather belts. It would have been interesting if they had not been such nasty looking men. I was terrified.

"One pirate was bigger than all the others and he wore a long frock coat with white lace at the cuffs. It looked odd because he wasn't wearing a shirt underneath and he very much needed a shave. He had gold rings in each ear and a colored kerchief around his head. He must have been the captain because he started giving orders and the others quickly rigged a long plank over the side of the ship.

"We were all wide awake but nobody spoke to us. Then, after a while, they grabbed Daddy and tied his arms behind his back. He fought so hard, it took four pirates to do it, and before they managed it, he had thrown one overboard. But finally, they got him onto the plank and pushed him off the end. There was a big splash and I screamed!"

"You sure did!" breathed her brother.

"Maybe that made them decide to take me next," she went on. "I struggled hard and hung on to a ring bolt close beside me on the deck. I screamed again and suddenly I was back here. I never thought I could be pleased to be back in a gloomy old tunnel, but I am. I'm glad Daddy is safe after all."

"What a harrowing experience, darling," murmured her mother, stroking her hair. "No wonder you screamed. I'm sure I would have done the same. Move closer to me. What are you holding there?"

"I'm still holding on to the ringbolt," replied Wendy sleepily.

# Chapter Fourteen

## THE TREASURE!

The Pallant family was used to hearing accounts of Wendy's lurid dreams, and it may be they no longer gave them full attention because it was Harry who saw the significance of her last remark.

"Ringbolt?!" he yelled. "Where?" Hurriedly focusing his light, he picked out Wendy's hand, half buried in powdered rock and dust.

A circular object was just visible, and as she quickly withdrew her hand, Harry began to clear away the debris.

"It's a ringbolt, all right," he crowed. "Good for you, Wendy! If you hadn't had that dream, we would never have found this."

The others were crowding around this.

"That's marvelous!" exclaimed the skipper. "Wendy must have been fidgeting about in her sleep and accidentally found the ringbolt. Whether finding it made her dream, or the dream made her find it is something we'll probably never know."

Pete joined his cousin in clearing the area around the ringbolt. "Get back, Mom," he cried. "I think there's a wooden trap door or something here."

Both boys used their hands like a dog uses his forepaws to dig a hole, while Mr. Pallant held his light steady on the area. Soon, they had uncovered a wooden trapdoor about two feet square.

The four youngsters began talking about getting out soon, but the skipper cautioned them not to count on it. "First we have to get that trapdoor open," he added. "And then we'll have a pretty good idea of what to expect down below. We want to go up, not down. We'll hope for the best, though."

The trapdoor was now thoroughly cleared and while his father was speaking, Pete had given a good hard pull on the ringbolt. Nothing moved. "It's solid!" he gasped.

"Let me have a try," the skipper stood astride the trapdoor and took a good grip of the ringbolt. Slowly, he exerted his full strength until perspiration beaded his brow. But the trapdoor showed no sign of movement. With a great gasp, he let go and sat down.

"I can't move it at all. We need some kind of bar to pass through the ringbolt so more of us can heave on it."

There was a short silence as everybody thought hard.

"What about the burned-out torch?" asked Wendy.

"Too short, I'm afraid."

"Would that old cutlass be of any use?" wondered her mother.

"It might, but it's a long way back along the tunnel."

"No, it isn't!" exclaimed Pauline. "I brought it along. It seemed such a wonderful souvenir. It's over here."

"Good for you, Pauline!" her father was really pleased. "Pass it over, lass."

The cutlass had a long, heavy blade and after using the point to clear around the edge of the trapdoor, the skipper passed it through the ringbolt.

"Now, you two boys take the handle between you and keep the back of the blade against the ring. I'll take the other end."

"You'll cut yourself, dear," put in his wife.

"Yes. I need something to form a pad," he stripped off his shirt and wrapped it carefully around the blade. "This will do nicely. Get set, boys."

The three braced themselves. "Heave slowly."

For probably the first time in their lives, the two boys exerted their full strength. Back muscles strained and lungs felt as though they would burst, until Pauline broke the tension: "It's moving!" she almost squeaked.

Sure enough, the heavy trapdoor was yielding at last. Slowly, the edges came clear and, rusty hinges protesting loudly, it pried open several inches.

"Enough boys!" gasped Mr. Pallant, his muscles gleaming with sweat. "Take a rest now, and then we'll get a hold of the edges and pull it open."

The boys promptly collapsed, but the girls were too excited to wait. Grasping the trapdoor, they started to heave, and their mother, almost as thrilled, joined them. But they could barely move it. The skipper took one side and the ancient hinges began to groan again.

Soon the trapdoor was upright and Pete quickly shone his light into the blackness below.

"Steps!" he crowed. "I knew this was the way out!"

Then they heard a noise which sent a chill through them all. A loud and distinct gurgle. Water!

The skipper shone his light farther down. Six stone steps ran down from the trapdoor. A seventh was just visible beneath the surface of the water.

"Steps down to nowhere," he said bitterly. "And yet, we shouldn't be surprised. We already knew there was water down below."

"But why go to all the trouble of making steps and a trapdoor if they didn't lead anywhere?" demanded Wendy.

"It doesn't make any sense," added her mother.

Mr. Pallant was silent for a moment. "You are right, there must be an explanation," he said at last. "Whomever did all this went to a lot of trouble and hard work, and people don't usually do that without good reason. Let's have another look."

Lying at full length on the ground, he directed his light down the steps again and studied them closely. "I think I have it," he said a little later as he rolled over and sat up.

"What is it, Dad?" asked Pauline eagerly.

"Three of the steps above the water level are wet, which shows that they were covered recently, until the tide started to go down. When the tide is dead low, we might learn why the steps were put there and where they lead."

"How long will that be?" Harry was obviously impatient.

"Between four and five hours to low water, but something could show up before then. We'll look down occasionally, but meanwhile, we may has well catch up on some sleep. We hadn't been asleep long before Wendy had us all captured by pirates!" He grinned at his little girl.

They each settled themselves as comfortably as possible by the flickering light of the torch in the wall. A little later, Pete broke the silence with: "Do you think it's time we looked at the steps again, Dad?"

"How long do you think it's been since we last looked, son?"

"Oh, about an hour, I suppose."

The skipper chuckled. "I doubt if it has been more than five minutes, but you can look if you like."

Pete switched on his light and peered down the trap door. "It hasn't gone down an inch." He exclaimed in disgust.

"It will be best if we all sleep for an hour or two," put in his mother. "Then it might be worth looking again."

They were all more tired than they realised, and it was not long before the only sound to be heard in the eerie tunnel was that of heavy breathing, plus an occasional gurgle of water.

Although he had lost all track of time, Harry's habit of early rising was still strong enough to awaken him at his usual hour. He had slept soundly, despite the hardness of his bed, but it took him quite some time to figure out where he was. The torch was now burning steadily, so the shadows were behaving more rationally, but even so, the tunnel was a startling place in which to wake up. The others were still asleep, and Harry might have dozed off again, had he not suddenly remembered the steps.

Taking his flashlight, he crawled quietly across to the trapdoor and shone a beam of light onto the steps. The tide was now well down, and another five steps were visible, but still they seemed to lead nowhere. He was about to turn away disappointed when his eye caught something beyond the steps and a little higher up. Focusing his light, he nearly fell down the trapdoor with excitement.

The top of a doorway cut into the rock face and a few inches of wooden door were showing above water level.

Harry sat up, too thrilled to keep quiet, but not wishing to wake the others. However, the problem was solved when his uncle asked softly, "What can you see, Harry?"

The boy was both startled and thankful. "There's a door down there," he breathed. "I knew those steps must lead somewhere."

The skipper moved quickly to the trapdoor and studied the top of the doorway carefully. Before he had finished, the others were awake and full of questions. When Harry told them what he had found, they all insisted on seeing it for themselves.

Pete ventured down the steps to have a closer look. "The tunnel underneath is similar to this one," he reported. "Except it's half-filled with water. There are only a few feet of rock between the two. The lower one has the same dead-end, but somebody put a door in it. Maybe it is a way out after all."

"That is difficult to imagine," said his father. "You don't usually open underground doors to step outside."

"Maybe it leads to another tunnel," said Wendy practically.

"That sounds possible," said her mother. "What else could it be?"

The skipper shook his head. "We can only guess, I suppose. But mine is that the door is watertight and leads directly into the treasure chamber. It is probably intended to be opened only at low tide, and is the 'back door' which the people who buried the treasure planned to use when they were ready to collect it. The door must be made of solid oak, or similar, because it looks to be in pretty fair condition even after all of these years."

"But weren't they expecting a lot for a wooden door to last for hundreds of years?" asked Harry.

His uncle could not resist the chuckle. "Would you bury treasure for hundreds of years, Harry? The only people who I can recall who buried treasure for long periods of time were Aztecs and the ancient Egyptians."

Now the boy looked puzzled. "What have they got to do with this treasure?"

"I get it!" said Pauline. "Most people would bury treasure temporarily until they could come back for it, some time later."

"Right!" agreed her father. "Nobody would go to all this trouble just to confuse future generations. They would more likely do it to prevent other people finding the loot before they were ready to use it themselves."

"So, whoever dug the pit must have known about the tunnels beforehand," suggested Wendy.

"I imagine so. And probably the other tunnels too."

"A fabulous treasure only a few feet away!" sighed Pauline. "And we won't even get to see it."

"Remember, it's only my theory," warned her father. "But if it is correct, you might say that we have discovered the secret of Oak Island! People have been searching for this since the treasure first became known."

"It won't be much use to us unless we find a way out of here," remarked her mother sadly. "What do we do next?"

The skipper thought for a moment. "There isn't much we can do, I'm afraid. Except to wait for the tide to uncover more of that door. It is just possible that we might be able to break it down."

They all settled down again, but with little hope of being able to go back to sleep.

"Thank Heaven that eerie sighing has stopped," observed Mrs. Pallant. "I kept imagining it was caused by a sleeping pirate who was bound to wake soon!"

"That's probably because the trap door is open, allowing the air pressure to equalize," said Pete loftily.

"Brilliant!" remarked Wendy solemnly.

"Obvious!" said Pauline.

Harry had to laugh. "Having sisters must really be something!"

"It is," agreed Pete. "I find it best to ignore them, mostly, but they do make life a heck of a lot more interesting. Anyhow, I just thought of something." Getting to his feet, he went to the wall and examined it closely. "Dad, where would this tunnel go if it didn't stop here?"

His father looked puzzled for a moment. "I suppose it would run straight into the Money Pit, as it is called. By thunder!" He jumped to his feet. "Most of that pit was dug out years ago. Maybe we could get out that way!"

"How?" Mrs. Pallant sounded doubtful.

"Well, I don't think we are very deep down, and if we can break though into the pit shaft, we could then shout for help. People on top would be bound to hear and they could lower something down and haul us to the surface." The skipper gave a sudden chuckle. "What a shock they would get seeing us coming out of the shaft, especially when we apparently never went down!"

Pauline giggled. "They would wonder why we weren't dressed in pirate clothes!"

"But how are we supposed to break through a rock wall?" asked her mother practically.

The skipper looked serious. "I am afraid that is the problem. We need a pickaxe, or something similar. It's a pity those pirates, or whoever they were, didn't leave a few tools behind."

"What about the cutlass?" asked Pete.

"That might do. It has a good, heavy blade. A lot will depend on how hard the rock is, and how thick."

Picking up the heavy weapon, he stabbed tentatively at the end wall. "It's pretty soft," he announced as chips of rock flew in all directions. "Maybe we are on our way out at last," he continued happily, "Thanks to Pete, the boy with the brains!"

"Oh dear!" sighed Pauline. "We shall never hear the last of this!"

But everybody suddenly felt cheerful as the skipper dug steadily at the rock face. After about fifteen minutes, he handed the cutlass over to Pete. Who also worked for fifteen minutes, before Harry to his place.

Mrs. Pallant and the girls insisted on taking turns, despite the weight of the tool and the fact that the point was now fairly blunt. In little over an hour, there was a sizeable hole cut two feet deep into the rock.

Harry was hacking away again, and the skipper had just remarked that he was sure they would break through very soon, when there was a dull boom and the whole tunnel shuddered violently, showering them all with dust.

"Run for it, everybody!" he roared. "They are using dynamite!"

But before they could even turn, there was a shattering roar and the end wall of the tunnel disappeared.

For a split second the flickering torch illuminated the inside of the Money Pit, showing hanging wooden supports dangling awkwardly.

Then they were almost blinded by a flash of orange flame as the detonation took full effect in the confined space.

During the fleeting instant of that searing flash of light, a colossal wooden chest appeared, as if to hover, floating in the chamber momentarily, apparently thrown up from the endless bottom of the Money Pit.

It burst open before their startled gazes.

A cascading wall of gold plate, thousands of ancient golden coins, and a dazzling jewelry display of rubies, sapphires, emeralds, pearls, and diamonds, all sparkled brilliantly in the bright dynamite explosion fireball. Every last sliver of riches all plummeted down the Money Pit shaft and out of sight, along with the remains of the treasure chest.

With that deep, great rumble, thousands of debris smithereens of wooden splinters, rocks, pebbles, and dust scattered onto the family.

Then all was sheer blackness.

The torch had been blown out by the sudden blast of air, and before anyone could make a move, they felt the rock floor crumbling beneath their feet.

They were falling, falling.

There was a loud splash, and then...

Silence.

*Bertram Smith*

# Chapter Fifteen

## *ANOTHER SHOCK.*

Harry found himself submerged in cold water and instinctively began to struggle to reach the surface. Seconds later he was gasping for air in darkness which seemed even more intense than previously.

"Is anybody here?" he called in a shaky voice.

"I am," came the welcome voice of his uncle, and at that moment, they were suddenly surrounded by splashing and glurping sounds. His aunt and the two girls soon identified themselves, and, as they did so, the water began to glow with some kind of illumination from below. Then Pete popped up with his lighted flashlight held in one hand.

"Glug!" he gulped. "Now I know this flashlight really is waterproof! I had it in my hand, but don't remember switching it on."

The others, temporarily blinded by the bright light, were relieved to know that nobody was missing. They were all bobbing up and down in the current of the underground river.

"Thank God we are all still alive!" Mrs. Pallant exclaimed, unable to repress a sob.

"It does seem like a miracle that we are," agreed her husband. "Is anybody hurt?"

"I think I took a rock into my shoe," put in Wendy.

On being assured that nobody was truly hurt, he went on: "They must have been blasting the Money Pit to get at the treasure."

"Did you see, Dad?" cried Pauline, suddenly remembering. "The chest, and all that treasure spilling out!"

"I did!" announced Pete, sounding somewhat awe stricken.

"Me too!" put in Wendy. "What a sight!"

"I think we all did," said her father. "And it was a fantastic sight! Not many people will even believe it ever really happened. That explosion must have shattered the chamber, and the treasure is now probably spread all around in the mud and debris. I doubt if they have gained anything."

"Nevermind the treasure," interrupted Mrs. Pallant. "What are we going to do now? We'll freeze to death in this water."

"We are going to swim for it. I don't know how far we have to go, but we are already moving in the right direction with the tide. Show the light around a little, Pete."

The light showed they were drifting close together along a tunnel about six feet wide, with the roof varying in height between one and several feet above their heads. Walls and roof glistened wet and black in the bobbing light.

"Where is the hole we fell through?" asked Harry.

"Some distance back, I hope," responded his uncle. "We seem to be drifting steadily, but if we swim, we should get out quicker as well as keeping warm. Take it easy though. Let the tide do the work. We'll take it in turns to hold the light. And the one holding it can lead the way. Off you go, Pete. We'll soon be back onboard the *Seawolf!*"

Feeling considerably cheered, they set off at a steady pace behind Pete. Who was swimming with just one hand. He found it awkward, but not really difficult, although the light bobbed around a lot and made the tunnel seem even more weird.

"It doesn't seem so cold when you are swimming," remarked Harry as he took over the flashlight a little later.

"That's true," agreed his aunt. "Incidentally, I suppose we are all in the situation we would have been in had we all fallen through that tilting stone trap."

"Except for one thing," said the skipper. "Then the tide was rising, and we would have been swept up the tunnel, with little chance of survival."

"Two things to be grateful for," put in Wendy, cheerfully swimming along. "Everybody can swim, and the tide is on our side!"

Pauline was feeling brighter too. "I just thought of something. We are in the middle of a thrilling adventure! My diary is going to make exciting reading!"

"I wish I was writing in my journal aboard the *Seawolf* right now," said her brother. "It would be so cosy."

"Yes, I've noticed before that adventuring can be quite uncomfortable," agreed Mr. Pallant. "I've never been one for the pipe, slippers, and easy-chair business, but right now, I'd sure be glad of the opportunity!"

"Surely it can't be much farther now," said his wife. "Here, you take the flashlight for a while."

As the skipper moved into position to take the lead, he gave an exclamation as his head caught against the roof. "Hold it, everybody, the roof is getting very low."

"It comes all the way down," put in Harry as the light showed the roof disappearing into the water just a few yards ahead.

"It does indeed," agreed his uncle, steadying the light. "This is something I was afraid of, but hoped wouldn't happen."

"Now what do we do?" Mrs. Pallant could not help sounding worried. "Can't we get out this way after all?"

"I am convinced we can get out with the tide, but we will have to wait until it gets a little lower." As he was speaking, he was extending his arm along the roof under water. "The roof goes only a few inches below the surface here, and if it is no lower farther along, then we should be able to carry on. Try holding on to the walls for a while."

Wendy gave a little scream. "Ugh! I tried and it's all slimy!"

"So it is," agreed her brother, holding on to a spur of rock as though it was the most comfortable support in the world.

"Boys have no sense of feeling," said Pauline after touching the wall gingerly. "I'm going to stretch out and float for a while."

"I can swim under water," put in Harry. "Shall I go find out if the roof rises again soon?"

"No, you will not," declared his uncle emphatically. "Suppose it doesn't rise again. You wouldn't be able to surface and it is doubtful if you could make your way back against the tide."

Meanwhile, Pete had swum as far as possible to examine the roof close to the surface of the water. "The water has gone down a fair amount already," he announced. "It won't be long now."

Without realizing it, he had spoken with his mouth close to both the water and the roof, and everybody was startled to hear a deep, rolling echo.

*"IT–WON'T–BE–LONG–NOW-ow-ow."*

"Listen to that!" chuckled Pete. "Now we know for sure it won't be long!" Putting his mouth to the narrow gap again he shouted, "Ahoy!"

Back it rolled with the booming voice of a giant. *"AHOY-oy!"*

"Let me try," said Wendy, swimming nearer. She shouted her name, but it came out much more squeaky than she had intended and the merciless echo threw back with a magnificent, shrill, *"WEENDEEEE-eee!"*

Everybody else had to laugh, then Harry moved into position and sent out a ghostly chuckle. It sounded awful as he made it, but the echo seemed ten times worse when it rolled back, hollow and eerie, *"WHOO-HOO! HA! HA! HA-ha-ha!"*

"Good Heavens, Harry!" exclaimed his aunt. "No more please. That would scare a ghost!"

Without any warning, Pete suddenly burst into song. *"Oh, for a life in the ocean wave,"* he caroled, setting off a confusion of echoes.

"*ON* the ocean wave you mean," corrected Pauline.

"IN, is correct here. Up to our necks!" insisted Pete. He was about to continue, but was interrupted by a shout from Harry.

"I can see some daylight!"

"Where?" everybody spoke at once.

"Put the light out, Pete, and look along the surface of the water."

Sure enough, with the lights out they could distinguish a faint, greenish glow between roof and water.

The skipper swam close and brought his eyes level with the surface of the water. "It's the entrance!" he cried. "The cave is only a few feet away. We must be on the other side of the wall where we saw that water disappearing underground."

Everybody laughed happily with the release from the entire night of tension.

"So our dinghy isn't far away," said Pauline.

"That's right, and we'll soon be in it," agreed her father happily. "We should be able to swim under water now. I'll go first and call back if it's O.K."

"Be careful, dear," put in Mrs. Pallant.

"Yes, dear."

"If it is all right, I'll send the children out and follow last." She put in.

Using the roof to push himself under, her husband disappeared into a swirl of water. The others waited tensely while seconds dragged like minutes. Their hearts jumped when a voice boomed through the narrow gap.

"All clear. Come through one at a time."

Harry went through next and found the green gloom of the cave bright compared with the blackness of the tunnel, making him blink hard.

"Over to the steps in the corner," directed his uncle.

The boy swam across as the others began to pop up one at a time. Reaching the steps, he was startled to see the dinghy in a vertical position with its stern barely touching the water.

"What's the matter with our boat?" asked Wendy as she joined him. The others were close behind and her father quickly spotted it.

"Ha! You must've tied her up too tight, Pete. You didn't allow for the fall of the tide."

"Well, I didn't know we were going in there to stay!" protested Pete. "I expected to be back in an hour or two."

"Of course, never mind. There's no harm done. I can ease her down into the water without any trouble." Climbing to the top step, the skipper slacked the mooring line gradually, and soon the dinghy was on an even keel alongside the steps.

"Get in everybody, gently, please."

Cold, wet, and shivering, they stepped carefully into the little boat and Mr. Pallant took the oars. "Cast off, Pete."

When they maneuvered through the entrance from the semi darkness of the cave into the comparative light of the overgrown stream, they were able to see each other properly for the first time in eighteen hours.

"Good Heavens!" exclaimed Mrs. Pallant. "What a fright we all look. Dirty, disheveled, and bruised. And your leg has been bleeding, Wendy."

"I never even felt it," said Wendy, looking with surprise at a deep scratch on her calf. "Might have something to do with that rock in my shoe that won't go away."

"I guess we are all a little battered," agreed her father. "We are very lucky to have escaped serious injury, and it was probably only the immediate ducking in cold water which prevented us all from suffering from shock after that explosion. We'll all be O.K. after a good clean-up and some rest. And food of course."

"Food!" exclaimed Pauline. "Oh, Heavenly thought. In a few minutes we shall be eating!"

Her father chuckled as he maneuvered the boat carefully. "I know how you feel and I wish I could offer you some hot soup right now—special dishrag soup!"

"Here we are," called Pete from the bow as they reached the mouth of the stream. "Down, everybody."

They all bent low as Pete grasped the branches overhead and pulled the boat through. It shot out into the sunshine so brilliant that they were all temporarily blinded.

"Oh, such wonderful warmth—" began Mrs. Pallant, but she was interrupted by a yell from Pete.

"Where is she? Where is the *Seawolf?!*"

His father twisted around so quickly he almost upset the dinghy and then they all stared in silent disbelief.

The *Seawolf* was nowhere in sight.

"Oh, no!" exclaimed Mrs. Pallant. "Not this, after all we've been through."

"She must have sprung a leak and sunk," said Harry sadly.

"If she had, her mastheads would be showing above the water, especially at low tide," replied his uncle. "I'm afraid she has been taken out of the lagoon."

"But why wasn't she tied up properly?" demanded Mrs. Pallant.

"Four mooring lines couldn't possibly slip at the same time. However, we'll check one as a matter of interest. The port bow line was made fast to that tree at the end of the beach. Let's have a look at it."

He headed the dinghy over to the small beach and ran it aground.

Peter stepped out into the shallow water and made his way through the bushes to the tree. "The rope is still made fast here," he announced.

"I suspected it might be," said his father. "Now let's see what the other end is like."

The thick rope was lying on the bottom, and Pete quickly hauled it ashore.

"It's been cut!" he exclaimed as the end came into view.

He brought it over the dinghy and they all examined it closely.

The rope had obviously been cut with a sharp knife.

# Chapter Sixteen

## *THANKS TO PIP!*

"Now what do we do?" asked Pauline wearily as they stepped out onto the little beach. "I'm awfully hungry."

"We all are, I'm afraid," said her father. "This is a terrible setback. I suppose we'll have to walk across the island and try to get a boat back to the mainland. Then we can call Anita for help, but first, we must have a rest and a dry-out."

Mrs. Pallant stretched out on the sand with a high sigh of relief, too exhausted even to worry. "This sand is so nice and soft, and the sun so warm. What a wonderful change from that dreadful tunnel and the cold water."

There was just enough room for them all to sprawl comfortably on the beach, and soon they began to feel drowsy in the unaccustomed warmth.

But the peace was suddenly shattered by Wendy who sat up with a wail. "What happened to Pip? I've just remembered we left him to guard the *Seawolf!*"

The others began to look worried as they thought of their beloved dog. What could have happened to him? They did not have to wonder for long. Wendy's voice had carried farther than she realised because there came a faint reply in the distance.

"EE–OW–OO!"

The cry of a lost dog.

"Did you hear that?" cried Wendy. "It's Pip!"

The others sat up, listening intently. Again, they heard the plaintive cry. "Pip!" yelled Wendy. "Come on, boy!"

They all heard an answering bark and the what sounded like a heavy splash.

"I wonder where on earth he could be!" worried Pauline.

"Listen!" put in her father. "That is either an elephant or Pip coming through the brush!"

Everybody laughed with relief as the crashing noise drew nearer. Then a very wet and excited dog burst into their midst. Pausing only to shake himself vigorously and give them all a quick shower, he hurled himself at Wendy and almost knocked her flat on her back. Whimpering with joy at finding his loved ones again and wagging his tail so furiously it was almost a blur, he licked her face rapidly and then jumped on Pauline. He was not satisfied until he had treated everybody the same, and then stretched out, panting.

"This is one time I really wish Pip could talk," commented the skipper. "I sure would like to know what happened to our boat, and why."

"Maybe those men on the black motor boat came into the lagoon, cut the ropes, and then they towed the *Seawolf* away," suggested Harry.

"That seems both possible and likely," agreed his uncle. "But why... *why?* I know they warned us to stay off the island, but taking our boat would be more likely to keep us on it. And if they did take it, where did they leave it, and how did Pip escape? Questions without answers, I am afraid."

Wendy got to her feet and stretched luxuriously. She was about to say something when she noticed Pip. He had risen when she did and headed straight into the bushes he had earlier emerged from. "What's the matter with Pip?" she asked.

As she spoke, the dog reappeared, barked, wagged his tail and then turned back into the bushes. A moment later, he came out again, barking and prancing around excitedly.

"Maybe he wants us to follow him," said Pauline.

"By thunder! I believe you're right!" exclaimed her father, jumping to his feet. "Come on, everybody, let's see if he does."

Pip gave a loud bark of pure delight when his family showed enough sense to do what he wanted them to do. He shot back into the undergrowth and soon they were having difficulty in forcing a way through behind him.

The skipper took the lead and the others followed in single file. "Now we are in the jungle," commented Pete. "Talk about adventuring!"

"I hope Pip doesn't have far to take us," said his father as he pushed his way through a particularly dense patch which the dog had slipped underneath.

A few minutes later, they burst suddenly out of the bush and onto the rocky shore and stood speechless. In front of them was the *Seawolf*, about thirty feet off shore, lying over on her starboard side at an angle of forty-five degrees. Both a welcome and an alarming sight!

"Whatever is the matter with her?" asked Mrs. Pallant in dismay.

"She's aground. High and dry," replied her husband. "I hope she isn't damaged. Come on. Let's wade out to her."

The water was little more than a foot deep around the boat.

"Ah, a sandy bottom," commented the skipper as he dug his toes into it. "I was afraid these rocks might continue this far out. There is a chance she isn't damaged after all."

"Poor old *Seawolf*," commented Harry as they all walked slowly around the hull. "She looks something like a stranded whale from this angle."

"No sign of damage," exclaimed his uncle happily. "I'll check inboard now." He scrambled up the sloping deck and disappeared into the cabin.

The others could hear him moving around as they waited anxiously. Soon, he appeared in the cabin doorway and announced cheerfully, "No damage inside either. She should float off safely with the tide, providing the weather remains calm. Come on board everybody. We can at least clean up and have something to eat."

"Hurrah for food!" cried Wendy as she led the others in a mad rush. Past tribulations were already forgotten as they clambered laughingly and awkwardly along the sloping deck into the crazily tilted cabin.

"How long before she will float again?" asked Mrs. Pallant, helping Pip onboard.

"Three or four hours," replied her husband. "The tide is just beginning to flood. We'll have some food and a couple of hours rest, and then see about getting her clear."

"This is like living in a crazy, mixed-up world!" chuckled Pete as he tried to find somewhere level on which to rest a plate. The table was useless and they were having to crawl around on the backs of the settees.

His mother had somehow managed to prop the stove upright and balance the kettle. "If ever I knew an occasion which called for a good hot drink of tea, this is it," she said gaily. "It's almost as good as being back in our own house."

In a surprisingly short time, she was passing steaming mugs around.

"Ah!" Pauline exclaimed. "My life is saved!"

It seemed as though the four would never eat their fill, but eventually they had to stop and by then the *Seawolf* was beginning to stir uneasily as the incoming tide flooded around her.

"Now, we can all rest for an hour or two," said the skipper. "Then, as soon as she floats, we'll take her back into the lagoon and tie up for a real rest."

With one side of the boat useless, they had some fun trying to find places in which to make themselves comfortable but eventually they all settled along the starboard settees in both cabins.

Mr. Pallant took up position nearest the door. "This will have to do for now. We can sleep later."

But they were all completed exhausted, and being dry and warm and full of food, sleep claimed them quickly. An hour and a half later, a grinding bump shook the boat and woke the skipper. The *Seawolf* was almost on an even keel, and he leapt up with a roar, "All hands on deck! We're afloat."

He dashed out on deck, followed by Harry who had been sprawled next to him. They found that the boat was being pushed up on the beach by the rising tide and beginning to grind her starboard bow against rock.

Jumping down into the cockpit again to start the motor, the skipper glanced into the cabin to see what had happened to the others. They were all still fast asleep. Even Pip had not stirred from his position near Wendy.

"Let them rest," he said to Harry. "We can handle this little job." Putting the motor in reverse, he held his breath for a moment and then let a sigh of relief as the *Seawolf* responded and began to slide smoothly off the beach.

It took only a few minutes to run around to the lagoon entrance and soon Harry was busy joining the ends of the severed moor lines. "Good work," said his uncle approvingly. "Now we can wake the others and tell them to go to bed!"

None of the others would believe that the boat had been moved without them knowing, and they all had to go on deck to see for themselves.

"Good!" exclaimed the mate. "Now we can have a real sleep. That was just an appetizer."

For once, there was a complete agreement on the subject of going to bed, and a few minutes later the only sound to be heard inside the *Seawolf* was that of Pip snoring.

It was early morning before anyone stirred. "Over twelve hours of solid sleep," marveled the skipper as he looked at his watch. "What a wonderful feeling!"

"Who's for a swim?" asked Harry. "It's a glorious, warm day." A few minutes later they were all splashing happily in the shady lagoon, and Pip lost no time in joining them. Unfortunately, his idea of swimming was to climb onto somebody's back, so everybody tried to keep out of his way.

Next came a hearty breakfast.

"What do you think happened to the *Seawolf* while we were in the tunnels, Dad?" asked Pete as they were eating.

"I can only guess that somebody came into the lagoon with a boat, cut our mooring lines and towed her out into open water before setting her adrift. I have no idea how far they took her, but after she was abandoned, local currents probably drifted her back inshore on a falling tide. Luckily for us, she grounded not far from here, but even so, we might never have known if it hadn't been for Pip. He probably prevented anyone from boarding her too."

"Good old Pip," said Wendy, rubbing the dog's ears. "I think he's really earned a place as a member of the crew."

"No doubt about that," agreed her mother. "In fact, he's proven to be a regular seadog."

"What happens next, Dad?" Pauline wanted to know.

"Well, I suppose we should go around to the other side of the island and tell those treasure hunters exactly what happened when they used the explosives. After that, we'll sail back to Halifax. Anita may be getting worried. We told her we would only be away one night."

"I wonder what they will say," Harry said with a chuckle. "Maybe they will think you are another crank!"

"I suppose it will sound a little far-fetched," agreed his uncle thoughtfully. "It will be difficult to prove, too. Unless they are prepared to come around to this side of the island and go into the tunnel with us."

"They certainly won't go into the tunnel with me!" asserted the first mate. "Nor with anyone else. Nothing will make me go near it again, ever!"

"Perhaps they will take my word for it," said her husband. "Anyhow, we'll soon find out. I think it might be wise though to go well out to sea to get around the island, just in case that motor boat is still nearby. Let's get under way."

The weather was ideal for sailing, and after steering clear of the lagoon, the skipper gave the order to hoist all sails. The four leapt to obey like veteran seamen, and soon the *Seawolf* was making good speed as she heeled slightly and lifted to the gentle Atlantic swell.

"What a change from dark tunnels, wet or dry," remarked Pauline as she stretched herself out comfortably on the warm, sunny cabin roof.

Half an hour later, Harry, who was idly using the binoculars, picked out a low, fast-moving object coming around the far end of the island. After watching it for a few moments, he announced: "Uncle, there's that black motor boat torpedo again. Coming our way."

The skipper took the glasses and studied the approaching boat carefully as it rapidly grew closer. "I think we'd better ignore it," he said. "Carry on as though you hadn't seen it."

But the black boat was not to be ignored so easily. It slowed down as it came near, and then circled the *Seawolf* as though to identify it. There was no one on deck as the big craft moved slowly by, although some figures could be seen inside the wheelhouse.

Suddenly, the powerful motors took on a deep roar in response to throttles opened wide, then the sleek hull rose half out of the water as the triple propellers exerted maximum thrust.

"They are going away," said Wendy with satisfaction.

"No, they are not!" cried her mother in horror. "They are coming straight for us!"

Everyone watched in fascination as the knife-like bows of the boat, riding high on a white wave, pointed straight at them.

*Bertram Smith*

# Chapter Seventeen

## *MORE TROUBLE.*

For one terrifying moment it seemed as though the black speed boat would ram the schooner amidships. But, at the very last moment, the high bows veered sharply and the powerboat cut across the path of the *Seawolf,* barely clearing her bowsprit.

There was a brief glimpse of leering faces through the windows of the wheelhouse and then the boat was clear, leaving a huge wave which made the schooner rear like a bucking horse.

Pip was standing on the foredeck barking furiously at this noisy intruder when they dived suddenly into the trough, scooping up a large part of the Atlantic Ocean, Fortunately, everyone was on the cabin top, so all they had to do was draw their feet up and hold on tightly. Not so for Pip. His bark was cut off sharply when a green wave swept on board and engulfed him. With a surprised look frozen on his face, he was swept along the port side-deck.

"Pip!" screamed Wendy as she saw him go by.

Her scream succeeded in diverting her father's attention from the motor boat and, grasping the situation, he quickly leaned over and caught Pip by the collar. Dropping the dog unceremoniously into the cockpit, he turned back to the other boat.

"The fools," he snorted. "I suppose they are trying to scare us. I'd like to see them try that maneuver across our stern."

Pete looked surprised. "Why do you hope they'll do the same thing across our stern, Dad? Surely if we took a wave like over our stern it would flood the cockpit and probably the cabins too."

"Not necessarily, son. It would be worth the risk because I know a little trick which would teach these people a sharp lesson."

The motor boat was a quarter of a mile away by this time and beginning to turn. Soon it was heading for the schooner again.

"I think they *are* going to try it," said the skipper with a fierce gleam in his eye. Starting the motor, he snapped an order. "Quick, you two boys get the long tow-rope up onto the starboard deck amidships. Make one end fast and standby to stream the other one overboard slowly when I give the word. But not before."

Puzzled, the boys began moving the heavy rope from the cockpit. It proved to be no easy task with the *Seawolf* still rising and falling unevenly, but soon all was ready and they crouched on the wet side-deck awaiting further instructions.

The motor torpedo boat was now heading straight for the schooner again, bows rising high as she gathered speed.

"O.K. boys!" called out the skipper urgently. "Start streaming the rope overboard." As he spoke, he put the motor in gear.

The mate and the two girls, having nothing else to do, watched awestruck from the cabin roof as the motorboat roared towards them again at maximum speed. Half her keel was now out of the water and it looked as though she was about to leap clear over the *Seawolf.*

Again, timing it to a split second, she altered course only enough to just miss the stern of the schooner. At that moment, the skipper opened his throttle wide and the schooner surged forward, only just in time to avoid being swamped by the huge wave thrown up by a seventy-foot torpedo boat flashing by in seconds.

The long tow-rope had been lying just below the surface of the water, and the forward lunge of the schooner gave it a jerk just as three high-speed propellors passed over it. There were three almost simultaneous thuds as the thick rope snarled up the propellers and stopped them dead. Then came the scream of stripping gears followed by an increased roar from motors released of their load. This stopped abruptly when the motors were switched off and the excited voices could be heard in the sudden silence which followed.

The skipper had a wide grin on his face. "That fixed 'em! Let go this end of the tow-line boys. It's no use now, and we probably couldn't get it back if it was. Our friends will probably be very excited when they realised what happened, so we'd better not stay too close."

"What a disreputable and scandalous ending to a notorious vessel of a dubious nature," said Pete, still practicing with his new dictionary words.

The gap between the two boats was widening steadily as the *Seawolf* pulled away. The torpedo boat was now wallowing sluggishly and they saw two men go along to her stern and peer over it. One must have seen the rope and guessed where it came from because he pointed first into the water, and then to the schooner. Shaking his fist at them he shouted something. The words did not reach them, but the meaning was clear enough.

"What will they do now, Dad?" asked Pete.

"There isn't much they can do, except wait for a boat to tow them to harbor and a repair shop. Right now, they are as safe as if they were in prison, so I think we'll head for the mainland and inform the police. They will send out a towboat and decide what charges can be laid against such hoodlums."

Pip was having some difficulty in getting out of the cockpit, so Pete jumped down to help, while his father turned his attention to steering. Harry was facing aft at that moment and happened to glance at the torpedo boat. With a shout, he threw himself against his uncle, knocking him away from the wheel, and the pair of them hurtled down into the cockpit on top of Pete and the dog.

There was a splintering crash as the pieces of the steering wheel flew in all directions and then a sharp crack followed by a scream from Mrs. Pallant, "They're firing at us!"

Disentangling himself as quickly as he could, the skipper peered cautiously over the stern and saw a man on the deck of the motor boat sighting a rifle. There was another sharp crack and a bullet thudded into the planking of the schooner. At that moment two other men ran out on deck and grappled with the man holding the rifle. After a fierce struggle, they managed to tear it from his grasp.

"Thank goodness!" gasped Mr. Pallant. "That man must be mad. The sooner we get away from here, the better!"

Using the shattered steering wheel as best he could, he carefully opened the throttle and the distance between the two boats began to increase steadily.

"Now we really have a case for the police. And, by the way, Harry, thank you. You probably did save my life that time!" he said.

Feeling a little embarrassed, Harry turned to help Pip out of the cockpit. Pete was still gasping for breath after having had all of the wind knocked out of him when the other two landed on top of him. Then he noticed something which made him use what little voice he had managed to regain to yell, "Dad! We're on fire!"

Everybody turned sharply to see a thin stream of smoke trickling from under the hatch just behind the motor. "Get forward, everybody, quickly!" roared the skipper. "That last bullet may have hit the gas tank!"

While the others were moving forward, he grabbed the nearest fire extinguisher, but before he could use it there was a shattering explosion and the whole rear of the schooner was blasted open.

The skipper trained his extinguisher on the flames, and every other one on board was quickly brought to bear, but it soon became evident that their combined efforts were futile. The fuel tank had burst, and the stern of the boat as well as the surface of the surrounding sea were now covered in the flaming gasoline.

"It's no use!" shouted Mr. Pallant as he emptied the last extinguisher. "Get the dinghy over the side quickly, and put in a few things we are likely to need. I'll try to keep her head into the wind so that the flames don't work forward too quickly. Move!"

With sinking hearts, the others lifted the rubber dinghy over the rail and then rushed below to collect their most precious possessions.

Despite the heat of the fire and the smashed steering wheel, the skipper managed to head the *Seawolf* into the wind and then he began anxiously searching the horizon for other vessels. There was nothing in sight except the motor boat, now a mile away.

A few minutes later, they were all squeezed into the dinghy and the skipper pulled clear. Twenty yards away he stopped rowing and they all sadly watched the blazing schooner. The after end of the cabin was well ablaze by this time, and moments later the leaping flames caught the dry sails. With a roar they surged upwards and in just seconds the masts, sails, and rigging were one huge blast of flame roaring high into the air.

"Poor old *Seawolf!*" sobbed Pauline.

"Just like Old Spiff described it," murmured Harry in awe.

Spirits were about as low as they could be and the mate felt impelled to try to raise them. "Never mind," she said as cheerfully as she could. "Things could be worse. At least we are all safe. Boats can be replaced, but people can't. The real problem is how long we are going to be cooped up in this tiny boat."

"That is a good question," said her husband. "If it had been dark, the burning boat would probably have attracted lots of attention, but on a bright sunny day like this, I doubt if it will even be noticed."

An hour later, the *Seawolf* had been reduced to no more than a smoldering hulk lying very low in the water. They were all feeling terribly cramped, but the skipper had decided to stay near the schooner until the end before trying to row to Oak Island. Now, as the fire attacked the damp bottom timbers, clouds of thick smoke began to billow from the wreck, making the perfect distress signal.

Fortunately, Pauline had remembered to bring the binoculars and she was spending most of her time using them to watch for passing vessels. But apart from a few ships passing in the far distance, she saw nothing likely to be of any help.

"You would expect some fishing boats around here at least," observed Pete.

"Or some pleasure boats," put in Pauline, still searching. "Where is everybody?"

"That's life," commented her father. "If we were doing something wrong and wanted to conceal it, be sure the sea would be swarming with boats of all kinds. However, keep looking Pauline. Something will surely show up soon. If it doesn't, we are going to have a long row back to Oak Island."

The heat of the sun had begun to make them all feel drowsy in their cramped quarters, but Pauline kept up her regular scrutiny of the surrounding sea. Suddenly, she gave a yell which made the others sit up, wide-eyed. A puff of wind had parted the long curtain of smoke drifting from the smoldering wreck and revealed a small ship only half a mile away. It was heading straight for them.

"A ship!" exclaimed Pauline. "And it must have been in sight for a long time, but I couldn't see it for the smoke."

"We'll row clear and make sure they don't miss us," said the skipper, taking up his oars again. Soon the ship was in full view and they could see that it was a small steamer with engine and bridge aft.

She looked well-kept, with fresh paint and brass work gleaming in the sun. The watchers saw a quick puff of white steam leave the steampipe attached to her squat funnel, and then a sharp blast of her siren reached their ears.

"They've spotted us!" exclaimed the skipper. "That was to let us know. It won't be long now. I sure will be glad to get onboard and stretch my legs."

A few minutes later, they heard the sharp clang of the ship's engine room telegraph across the water as her captain rang down for the engine to be stopped.

"What kind of ship is it?" asked Harry cautiously.

"It's a little coaster," replied his uncle. "About a thousand tons, I would say. That is the kind of ship that I went out to sea in when I was just fourteen years old. She probably tramps up and down the coast looking for cargoes."

"How many crew would a ship like that carry?" wondered Pauline.

"Oh, about a dozen. Look! He's waving us alongside. Let's go."

"She's called the *Lulanga*," remarked Pete as they drew close enough to distinguish the white lettering on the ship's bow. Obviously fully loaded, she was sitting very low in the water and only a short rope was required to enable them all to scramble aboard. This was secured by two seamen who then helped each one climb over the bulwarks. The skipper came last after passing up Pip and all the loose gear.

"Grab the dinghy lads, and haul it inboard," called a deep voice from the bridge above. The two brawny sailors reached down, grasped one end each, and swung the dingy over the bulwarks with ease and set it down on the broad foredeck.

Meanwhile, Pip was scampering around, sniffing and trying to explore everywhere at once as quickly as possible. He was so busy checking the scuppers that he did not notice a huge black cat approaching. The cat had his eyes glued on him and it was obvious that an interesting situation was about to develop. Everybody in sight paused to watch.

Pip got the shock of his life when he looked up and found a cat almost as big as himself, only two feet away. His expertise with cats had been confined to chasing an occasional intruder from his backyard, and he had never known one to stop and argue. It did not occur to him that he was now the intruder, so he lunged forward, as usual.

The big tomcat arched his back quickly, but instead of turning to run, he sat back on his haunches and, as soon as Pip came within range, slapped the dog neatly on each ear with a front paw.

"How's that for a neat left and right!" exclaimed one of the seamen admiringly. "Good old Spike!"

Pip sat back in consternation. He had never had his ears boxed before and he was probably too stunned to do anything about it.

Satisfied that the intruder had been properly put in his place, Spike turned majestically and leisurely made his way forward. After just a moment's pause, Pip wagged his tail uncertainly and then followed at a discreet distance.

"That settled that," observed the captain from the bridge. "They'll probably be pals from now on!" Everybody was still chuckling when he continued: "Come along aft, you people."

They all filed up the steel ladder leading to the long poop deck and as they did so the captain descended the bridge ladder to meet them. He was a tall, slightly stooped man with gray hair and a ruddy face.

"I am Captain Sellers," he said pleasantly. "I see you had a bad fire. Anybody hurt?"

Assuring him that they were all in good shape, Mr. Pallant told who they were and what happened.

Captain Sellers looked grave. "This is serious. I'll have to report it to the police as soon as we dock. Unfortunately, our little radio is out of action again or I would do it now. I wondered why that motorboat hadn't gone to your assistance. We'll probably get a closer look at her as we go by in half an hour or so."

He turned as a burly man joined them. "This is my mate, Mr. Jeffrey Hall. See that these people get something to eat and a chance to clean up, Jeff. I'll get the ship back on course. See you later folks."

"I guess you've all had a pretty rough time," said the mate sympathetically. You men can use my cabin to clean up in, and the girls can use the captain's. I'll tell the cook to fix up a meal for you all while you are doing it."

He led them below to where half a dozen cabins opened from a narrow alleyway and, after making sure that plenty of towels and soap were available, left them to their big clean up.

The mate's cabin was very small with a polished wooden bunk running its full length. Above the bunk was the single porthole and below it, a set of built in drawers. A chair, a washbin, and a narrow clothes locker completed the furnishings, leaving barely enough room for the three guests to stand at the same time.

"Golly!" exclaimed Harry. "They don't have much room on these ships, do they?"

His uncle chuckled as he edged over to the washbin. "You should see the fo'c'sle accommodation provided for the seamen. They would probably think this is luxurious. The captain maybe does a little better, but not much."

They barely had time to remove the grime left by fire and smoke before the mate reappeared, calling for Mr. Pallant. "The captain would like to see you on the bridge. We are closing in on the motorboat and he thinks something has happened onboard."

"Tell your mother and the girls, Pete," said the skipper as he and Harry followed the mate up on the small bridge. The others arrived almost immediately, to hear the captain saying:

"Your boat finally sank, but I didn't call you because I thought you might like to be spared such a sad sight. But there is something else I am sure you will want to see." He pointed to where the big motor boat was rolling gently about a hundred yards away. There was no sign of life onboard.

"Have a look through these," the captain handed Mr. Pallant a huge pair of binoculars. Harry, who had picked up their glasses as he came on deck, immediately put them to his eyes, too.

"I can see two men lying on deck," announced Mr. Pallant after a moment. "Perhaps 'sprawled' would be a better word."

"That is exactly what I thought—" began Captain Sellers, but Harry quickly interrupted with: "One has a revolver in his hand!" Hurriedly, his uncle looked again. "By thunder, you are right. Here, take a look, Captain."

Captain Sellers took a long careful look. "They both have guns," he announced. "It looks as though these men might have had a shooting match and canceled each other out."

"That seems likely," agreed Mr. Pallant. "I told you we saw them fighting over a rifle. What do you intend to do?"

"Well, I don't have much choice. It is my legal responsibility as a ship's master to render assistance at sea. I'll have to go alongside that boat and find out if those men need medical aid. Then I may as well take it in tow." He began to give the helmsmen instructions to guide his sharp alongside the wallowing motorboat.

The two figures lying on deck did not stir as the *Lulanga* moved in close. As soon as his ship stopped, the captain directed two seamen to jump onto the deck of the boat and make her fast. Immediately the boat was secured and he went down to his own foredeck, climbed over the bulwarks and jumped on to the narrow side deck of the motorboat. Carefully, he made his way forward.

The nearest figure was sprawled awkwardly on its back with a gun clenched tightly in its right hand and Captain Sellers bent down for a closer look.

Suddenly, the man came to life, and the gun was pointed directly between the captain's eyes.

*Bertram Smith*

# Chapter Eighteen

## *A SCREAM!*

"Welcome aboard, Captain!" The man had a grin on his unpleasant face as he carefully got to his feet, keeping the gun trained on Captain Sellers.

The other man immediately sprang up and pointed his gun at the nearest seaman. "Come on, you guys!" he shouted. "Everything is under control."

The door of the small wheelhouse opened and three more ruffians came out on deck. Two were armed with revolvers while the third carried a sub-machine gun. This he promptly pointed towards the ship, where almost everybody was lining the rail to look at the motorboat.

The five gunmen were a tough-looking crowd, obviously very determined and capable, but Captain Sellers was more angry than scared. "What is the idea?" he roared. "You people are asking to go straight to jail."

The first gunmen, apparently the leader, laughed grimly. "That was a neat trick, eh, Captain?" he jeered. "We saw you rescue those people from the burning schooner and guessed they would advise you to keep clear of us. So a little play-acting seemed to be called for. And it worked just fine. Maybe I should go on the stage!"

Captain Sellers clenched his fists. For a moment it looked as though he might attack the man in spite of his gun. The mate, who was watching from the bridge, called anxious warning.

"Take it easy, Bob. They mean business."

"Spoke like a man of sense," said the gangster. "Now let's get onboard the ship. You up there," he added to the mate. "Assemble everybody on deck."

A few minutes later, everybody onboard the *Lulanga* was gathered on the poop deck and covered by five menacing guns.

The leader of the gang, a tall bony man with a hook nose, spoke up. "We intend to borrow this ship until tomorrow morning. She will anchor near Oak Island for the night, and everybody will be put under lock and key. If anybody gives trouble, they will get trouble. Otherwise, you can all have a good night's sleep and wake up to find us gone."

"You realise that this is piracy," snapped Captain Sellers.

The leader thought for a moment and then chuckled. "Yes, I suppose it is. I never expected to do anything like this. And to think how I wanted to be a pirate when I was a kid!"

The man's expression changed as he continued: "Whatever it is, it's necessary, so get your ship under way again. I want her anchored on this side of the island and your motorboat lowered into the water. After that it's everybody to his quarters. Anybody on deck tonight will be asking for a bullet."

"Just a moment," said Mr. Pallant. "I have something to say. What was the idea with attacking my schooner? She is a total loss and we were lucky to escape alive."

The gangster looked at him sharply. "So, you are the guy with the sailboat who got us into this mess. You and your trailing ropes. You must have done it on purpose."

Without any warning, he stepped forward and, using his gun as a club, struck the skipper on the side of the head.

Mrs. Pallant screamed as her husband slumped to the deck, then quickly knelt beside him. The four stared helplessly.

"Take these people away and lock them up somewhere," ordered the leader. "Lock them kids up too. We don't want them running all over the ship."

Two of the hoodlums put away their revolvers, and picking up Mr. Pallant began to carry him below while his wife walked anxiously alongside.

"You'll pay for this!" she said quietly.

"Come on, you kids," said another member of the gang. "Let's find a hole to put you in."

White-faced and quiet, the four were shepherded down a companionway to the deck below, where several doors opened off a bare alleyway.

"Here's one with a key in the door!" exclaimed their guard. "Just what we need. In you go, all of you, and I don't want to hear a peep from you all night."

He threw open the door and the four marched in silently. Then they heard a lock click behind them.

They found themselves in a small cabin lit by a single porthole. It had a built-in bunk and lockers, but judging by the boxes and cartons stowed everywhere, it was being used as a storeroom.

"Poor Daddy," choked Pauline, sitting on a carton. "That brute could have killed him!"

"Don't worry," her brother tried to be reassuring. "You know he's often said his head must be like wood because of the many hard knocks he has survived. I saw his eyelids flicker as they carried him away, so I'm sure he'll be all right. Especially as Mother is there to look after him."

"Where did they take him?" asked Wendy in a shaky voice.

"Somewhere on the other side of the ship, I believe," replied Pete. "Probably in a cabin like this one."

"So, all we have to do now is wait until tomorrow morning," put in Harry. "I wonder what is going to happen between now and then."

"I would give a lot to know," observed Pete. "Here we go again."

As he spoke, the engine started to throb and the *Lulanga* began to move ahead. "We may as well settle down for a while," he continued. "It won't take long to get to Oak Island. Let's move some of these cartons and try to make comfortable seats."

Harry grasped at the nearest one. "They are full of food!" Cans and cans of it. This must be a reserve supply or something."

"Food!" sighed Wendy, suddenly realising how hungry she was. "We were just going to have a meal, remember? If only we had a can opener!"

"I have on my pocket knife," said Pete. "I don't think Captain Sellers would mind. In any case, we can offer to pay for anything we take."

A few minutes later he had opened some cans of baked beans and one of ham, and they fell to with a will.

"Fingers were made before forks, as the saying goes!" chuckled Pauline.

Before they had finished their meal, the steady throb of the engine stopped and they heard the rattle of the anchor chain. There was a tramping of heavy feet on the deck above their heads and then silence.

"I suppose the crew is now being locked up," said Pete. "I wonder what is going to happen next. It won't be long before dark."

"Goodness! It's stuffy in here," exclaimed Pauline. "Can't we have that port open?"

"I don't see why not," said Harry. He crawled over the piled-up boxes and, after unscrewing the bolts, swung the big glass port upwards. A welcome, cool breeze immediately flooded into the cabin and Pauline was opening her mouth to express her appreciation when a man's voice reached them clearly through the porthole.

"You two had better get going with the motorboat and see how Jake is doing. It's only a small boat, so you might have to make two trips."

Harry held up his hand for silence. "They must be leaning against the rail just above us," he hissed. A few moments later they heard footsteps of two men walking away, and then came the sputter of a small motor which soon faded as the boat moved away from the ship.

The four in the cabin hardly dared breathe in case the man still standing above should hear them. How long was he going to stay there? Then Harry, who was crouching near the open port, saw a glowing cigar butt fall into the water. Heavy footsteps moved away overhead and could be heard continuing up the steps leading to the bridge.

"Thank goodness for that," breathed Pauline. "I thought he would never go away."

"He's on the bridge now," said Pete. "Probably keeping lookout."

"Listen!" exclaimed Harry. Four pairs of ears strained. "There's an aeroplane coming," he went on. "A small one by the sound of it." Cautiously, he put his head half through the porthole. It was now dusk and he soon picked out the red and green navigation lights of a small aircraft headed towards the ship. Pulling his head in quickly, he turned to Pete. "Have you still got your flashlight?"

"Yes, why?" asked his cousin, pulling his flashlight from his pocket.

"That plane is headed this way. How about if I signal S.O.S. as he passes?"

"Harry, you're a genius!" exclaimed Wendy.

"Good thinking," added Pete as he handed over his flashlight.

Keeping the beam as low as possible so that it could not be seen from the bridge, Harry directed it at the fast-approaching plane and rapidly clicked the well-known three short, three long, and three short flashes.

## *S.O.S!*

He just had time to repeat it once before the plane swept overhead with a roar.

"Do you think he saw the signal?" asked Pauline excitedly as Harry left his station near the porthole.

"It's impossible to say. The pilot was probably thinking of other things and, unless he happened to be looking straight at the ship at that moment, he might not see such a tiny light."

"Well, it was worth a try," Pete said. "Now all we can do is wait to see what happens."

"Talking of seeing," put in Wendy, who was stretched out comfortably on the only bunk. "Isn't there a light in this cabin?"

"There's a switch by the door," said Harry. "I'll see if it works."

"Hold on," interrupted Pauline. "If we put the light on it will shine through the port, and anybody on deck will notice it. If we stay in the dark and keep quiet, we might hear something important, and then we can tell the police later on."

"By Golly, she's right!" exclaimed Pete. "We might hear something worthwhile when the boat returns. We don't really need a light."

"Good for you, Pauline," observed Wendy.

Making themselves as comfortable as possible, the four settled down to wait. They were whispering quietly among themselves an hour or so later when Harry suddenly exclaimed, "Listen! Here comes the boat!"

The unmistakable sound of the ship's boat quickly became clearer and soon they felt it bump alongside. It tied up just forward of the cabin where the four were imprisoned and they heard the footsteps of the three men who had remained on board going to meet their accomplices.

"That you, Jake?" asked the leader.

"Yes," replied a voice the four had not heard before. There was a great deal of noise as the men clambered over the ships rail, and then the leader spoke again.

"Did you bring a load?"

"No, Ed. There isn't going to be any," replied Jake.

"What do you mean? Why not?"

"Those engineers must have made a miscalculation with their explosives. Instead of blasting the surrounding area clear, they blew up the treasure chamber. Everything in it probably went down into the mud at the bottom, and then the sides of the pit collapsed. So, now they are farther back then when they started. It will take months to get anywhere near the treasure again—that is if they ever do."

There was silence for a moment while the four listeners hardly dared to breathe.

"That's a shocker," said Ed at last. "I wonder what the 'Old Man' will say. He expects a big load to be ready for him tomorrow morning."

The four in the cabin were tingling with excitement.

"So they *were* after the treasure," whispered Wendy. "That explains things a little, anyway."

"Shh!" hissed Pauline as the voices started again.

The men had begun to express disappointment but the leader interrupted with, "Well, it can't be helped. It's not our fault. You guys can get something to eat if you like. Show them where the messroom is, Jim."

Four of the men tramped away and the listeners heard the scratch of matches as the others started to smoke.

"What time is *Pegasus* due, Ed?" asked the second man.

"Five o'clock. Just after dawn."

"Do you think the 'Old Man' will be very mad?"

"I don't think so. I believe the main reason for sending us on this job was to get us out of New York until things quieted down. That big bank job we pulled at Central Bank back in the Spring certainly stirred things up. With that money, plus what he made on the horses lately, I don't think he can complain. He might be upset when he hears that we had to abandon the motorboat, through."

"I don't suppose we can complain either," remarked the other man after a short silence. "It's been a holiday for us. But I won't be sorry to see the good old East Side again. So far as I am concerned, hunting pirate treasure is for the birds. There's enough treasure in little old New York, if you know where to look!"

The leader chuckled. "How right you are! Well, I suppose we'd better keep a lookout on this tub. We can't afford any last-minute hitches. I'll go up to the bridge."

"They must be a gang of big-time crooks," murmured Pete. "It's a pity we can't wreck their plans somehow."

"What can we do in a locked cabin?" asked Pauline.

"I think it would be fairly easy to get out," said Harry quietly.

"You do?" queried Wendy. "How?"

"That porthole is big enough for us to slide through, and it is only a couple of feet below the deck, so we could pull ourselves up by gripping the bottom deck rail."

"By Golly! That's a great idea!" exclaimed Pauline.

"We can't climb out with that man standing there," reasoned Wendy in a low voice.

"He won't be standing there all night," said Harry. "All we have to do is wait."

Pete spoke again. "I don't think the girls should come," he said doubtfully. "It might be dangerous."

There was silence for a moment. "Did you hear that, Pauline?" whispered Wendy.

"I did," replied her sister. "The poor sap doesn't realise that we have to go, if only to look after him!"

"He may be right," put in Harry. "We could always come back for you."

"Of course I'm factually accurate," agreed Pete, trying to sound grown-up with his dictionary words. "This is prominently distinguished gentlemen's work."

"In that case, we'll all stay here," quipped Pauline pointedly.

The man standing above their heads coughed suddenly and they all froze.

A moment later the quiet was shattered by the piercing scream of a woman.

*Bertram Smith*

# Chapter Nineteen

## *A CIGAR AND A GHOST!*

"What was that?" shouted the man on the bridge.

"I'll check," snapped the other, and the four heard him run across the deck.

"That must have been Mom!" worried Pauline. "What are they doing to her?"

"Let's find out," said her sister grimly. "That is if we really can get out of here."

"I have it all figured out," put in Harry quickly. "Here, help me build a launching platform with these cartons and make it level with the port. Then, all we will have to do is lie flat on our backs, reach out through the port, and pull ourselves halfway through. After that, we should be a be able to sit up, grasp the lower rail, and swing up on deck."

"I hope it will be that easy," Pauline sounded doubtful.

It did not take them long to build the platform and quickly agreed that Harry should go first. If he found the deck clear,

Pauline would follow, then Wendy, and finally Pete. There was no more talk about the girls not going.

Demonstrating his theory, Harry did it so well that he almost shot overboard. Catching himself just in time, he groped for the edge of the deck above and then for the lower rail. Hauling himself up without difficulty, he swung over the top rail and landed lightly on deck. As he had hoped, the deck was empty, although he knew that the lookout on the bridge might well be watching.

Carefully, the boy studied the bridge from his low angle of view. It stood out black against the starlit sky, but there was no human silhouette to break the stark outline. Putting his head under the lower rail and over the edge of the deck, Harry found that he could almost see into the cabin below.

"All clear!" he hissed.

In less than two minutes the others were standing by his side, hardly daring to breathe. Fortunately, the moon had not yet risen and the deck was deep in dark shadows.

Facing them across the deck was an open doorway faintly illuminated by a glow from the inside.

"Come on," whispered Pete and led the way towards it.

The doorway proved to be the entrance to the engine room, and the faint light came from a bulb glowing over the ship's generating unit far below. Sniffing the characteristic odor of steam mixed with oil, they peered down into a shadowy world of steel gratings connected by vertical ladders which disappeared among a faintly gleaming mass of machinery. Pipes appeared to run in all directions with the dim lighting making weird shadows among them. To the unaccustomed eyes of the four, the place looked more like a workshop on Mars than the engine room of a prosaic tramp steamer.

Pete was about to turn away when his eye caught something. Just inside the doorway was a tool rack fitted to the bulkhead. It contained a set of tubular spanners of various sizes.

"Just what we need," he whispered as he extracted one. "If I stick this in somebody's ribs it will feel just like a gun. We might be able to put a wrench into their plans after all. Let's go!"

Moving stealthily along the deck, they found the next door open. It seemed even blacker inside than out, and Pete put one hand over his flashlight before switching it on and off quickly. They had a brief glimpse of a huge cooking stove dominating the whole of the forward section. Obviously, this was the galley.

Slipping quietly inside, Pete put on his light again and then chuckled to himself. "The very things," he said as he directed his light on to a temporary washing line strung over the stove with several dry cloths hanging from it.

"What---?" began Wendy.

"You girls grab a cloth each," instructed her brother in a low voice. "And you take the line, Harry. When we find one of these men alone, this is what we'll do."

The others listened eagerly to his plan and then followed him carefully back on deck. With thumping hearts, they turned away from the bridge and crept towards the stern, hoping to find a single look-out stationed there.

Pete was about to peer around the corner of the deckhouse when they heard a man suddenly clear his throat. The four froze for a moment, but when nothing happened, Pete took a quick look. Sure enough, there was a stern look-out leaning against the rail with his back towards them.

Moving like shadows, the four slipped across the deck. The man stiffened suddenly as he felt something hard push against his lower back.

"Don't move!" said a menacing voice, which Pete hoped sounded deep enough.

Before the man had time to think, Harry had thrown a noose over his shoulders. As this was tightened, Pauline stepped forward and slipped a cloth over his mouth. Quickly she knotted it behind his neck and at the same time, Wendy passed the end of the line around the man's waist. Harry hauled it tight, and in a matter of seconds, the startled man found himself bound and gagged.

"Quick! Pull him over here and tie his feet!" whispered Pete. The others grabbed the prisoner with a will and moments later, he was safely secured and hidden behind a huge coil of rope.

"Nice work!" said Wendy jubilantly. "Let's try that again."

"Right on!" agreed Harry. "I've just found some more thin rope."

Thrilled at the success of their first attempt at kidnapping, they made their way stealthily around the deckhouse to the other side of the ship and then stopped.

Light was streaming across the deck from an open doorway only a few feet away. Signaling the others to stay where they were, Pete crouched low and edged silently forward.

Cautiously he glanced in at the lower corner of the doorway and then immediately returned to the others.

"What luck!" he whispered. "That is the messroom and two of the gang are stretched out on settees. They must be asleep or the racket would have brought them out by now. There is no other door, so if we could lock this one and take the key, we'd have them trapped!"

"That should be easy enough," said Pauline.

"Maybe," replied her brother. "You three stay here and leave it to me. If I get caught, I'll try to keep them busy long enough for you to find Mom and Dad." He slipped away before anyone could argue, and they saw him peep briefly into the messroom again.

The door was fastened back against the bulkhead away from him, and Pete realised that he would have to cross the shaft of light in order to release the catch. Dropping to his hands and knees and holding his breath, he passed the open doorway and groped for the catch behind the door. Easing it clear, he began to close the door. Luckily the key was in the lock, but a squeaky hinge or a noisy lock could disturb the men and they would then be able to shout and bang on the door to attract attention.

Much to his relief, he was able to close the door without a sound, and slipping the key into his pocket he rejoined the others. "That takes care of them for a while," he said with a grin.

"This is exciting," breathed Wendy. "Now what?"

"More hunting," said Pete. "Let's go!"

He led the way silently along the deck and paused to peer around the huge ventilator. "Watch out!" he hissed.

The others peeped around and made out a figure of a tall man standing with his back towards them.

"Same plan," ordered Pete and the others spread out, ready to repeat their previous performance.

"Don't move!" growled Pete as he jabbed with his spanner.

"Take it easy, son," whispered a familiar voice. "That gun barrel hurts. Where did you get a gun from, anyway?"

The four gasped together.

"Dad!" exclaimed Pauline. "What—where—?"

"Never mind that now. I'll explain later. Give me the gun, Pete."

"It isn't a gun," chuckled Pete as he handed over his weapon. "It's a spanner!"

His father laughed quietly. "Good for you, Pete. A real chip off the old block! I'll use it the same way, Now, you'd better find a safe place, all of you. There are six thugs on this ship. I've taken care of two and now I'm going after the others."

"We've got three!" squeaked Wendy gleefully.

"One tied up and two locked up," added Pauline proudly.

"You have?" Her father sounded incredulous. "You've done a wonderful job and you are one up on me. I couldn't be prouder of all of you. That leaves only the leader—the man who slugged me. I particularly want to deal with him myself."

"There's one!" exclaimed Wendy pointing to a glowing cigar below the bridge. Above the cigar they were able to make out the shape of a man's hat, but the rest of the figure was in deep shadow.

"Don't touch that one," said her father quickly. "That's your mother!"

For once, the four were all speechless at the same time.

"M—m—?" began Pauline.

"Yes. She's taking the place of a man I knocked out; in case the leader looks down from the bridge. If he does, he will think his man is still there, and that will give me a little more time to plan my attack."

The skipper edged quietly towards the fiercely glowing cigar, closely followed by the others.

"Mother!" giggled Wendy. "What are you doing?"

"Helping your father, as usual!" choked Mrs. Pallant as she removed the cigar from her mouth. "Ugh! How can men enjoy smoking these things? They're awful!"

"The hat suits you," grinned Pauline, peering closely at the felt hat perched on her mother's wavy hair.

"Stick it out, old girl," whispered Mr. Pallant encouragingly. "You are doing just fine. Now, I want you to stand at the bottom of the bridge steps. I will shout to the man up there and then slip around to the steps on the other side. When he comes to this side to see why he was called, you start climbing the steps slowly. Don't say anything, but keep the cigar going full bore."

"Ugh!" she said again. "Be careful, dear."

"Meanwhile, I'll be able to get up the other steps and hopefully catch him from behind. O.K.? Keep out of sight, you four."

Standing at the bottom of the steps leading up to the bridge, the skipper called out in a loud voice, "Hey Ed!" Then he slipped away, leaving his wife standing there.

The four were out of sight under the bridge wing and they heard the man above walk over to the top of the steps.

"What do you want, Jeff?" he asked.

Mrs. Pallant gave the cigar an extra big puff, choked slightly, and started slowly up the steps.

The leader stood waiting patiently until, a few moments later, he received the shock of his life as a pair of hands closed around his throat with a paralysing grip. Terror stricken; his hands involuntarily flew to his neck. Then he found himself lifted clear off the deck.

The listeners below heard something plop into the sea alongside the ship and then, "Now, let's see what kind of man you are without a gun!" It was the skipper's voice with a hard edge that none of them had heard before.

There came sounds of a scuffle and some heavy breathing followed by a couple of thuds, and then in a jubilant tone, "Stand clear below."

The steps leading up to the bridge were narrow and each side had a polished brass handrail on. Draping the unconscious gangster across these handrails, the skipper simply let go. Slowly, the man slid down, to land on the deck with a thud.

"Good for you, Dad!" chuckled Pete.

"Tie him up, boys. You can throw the cigar away now, Ivy."

With a sigh of relief, Mrs. Pallant tossed the cigar overboard as her husband descended the bridge steps. "That's three each," he announced with satisfaction.

Suddenly Pauline remembered. "Are you all right, Mom?" she asked anxiously. "We heard the most awful scream, and thought it must be you."

"It was!" smiled her mother. "Did it sound awful? That's good! It was meant to, but I've had no experience at screaming for help, so I wasn't sure how it would sound. I must admit, it did produce the result I'd hoped for."

"It sent chills down our spines," Wendy assured her. "In fact, that is what made us try to escape."

"It also gave us the opportunity," put in her brother.

"Well, it looks as though things worked out just fine," said the skipper. "I got very bored sitting in that cabin, so I decided to try to get out and free the crew. The porthole was too small for a grown-up to get through, so it had to be at the door. I know that one thing is always sure to attract a man's attention is the scream of a woman—the more agonising, the better. Your mother would have made a fantastic actress!"

"It worked perfectly," said Harry in admiration. "We heard the man on the bridge shout to the one who was standing on deck just above our cabin. He went off in a hurry to find out about the scream, which left the coast clear for us to escape."

"Yes, I was counting on only one man answering," said his uncle.

"But what actually happened?" demanded Pauline impatiently.

Her mother took up the story. "The man came to our cabin door and shouted through to ask what was wrong. I gave a couple of heartbroken sobs, put a quaver in my voice and told him that my husband had been trying to get through the porthole and got himself stuck halfway. Would the man help, please? He muttered something nasty, unlocked the door and marched in. He got an awful shock when he found your father waiting for him!"

"He was out cold before he had time to change his expression!" chuckled the skipper. "Then we prowled around, trying to find where the crew members were locked up, but we stumbled on another member of the gang. I dealt with him too, but he was in sight of the bridge, so I persuaded your mother to take his place for a while. I was just considering my next move when you four showed up. You've done a marvelous job, but what happened exactly?"

Four voices began to speak at once and Mr. Pallant had to hold up a hand to stem the torrent of words. "Only one, please, Pete, you tell us."

Pete quickly described what had happened to them and mentioned the conversation they had overheard through the open port.

When he had finished, his father whistled softly and said: "Now we are beginning to get some idea of what has been going on. It sounds as though a gang of New York crooks is after the treasure, and we spoiled things by putting their boat out of action. I don't understand why they picked on us in the first place, though."

"What are we going to do next?" wondered Harry. "This *Pegasus*, whatever it is, is due about five o'clock and it's past three now."

"*Pegasus*," repeated his uncle thoughtfully. "That has a familiar ring. Oh, yes, of course. *Pegasus* was the winged horse of Greek mythology."

"A horse that flies!" said Wendy. "That should be worth seeing!"

"That man said something about his boss making a lot of money on horses," volunteered Pauline.

"He did, eh?" Her father scratched his chin thoughtfully. "Well, I don't suppose Wendy will get to see a real flying horse, and I can't imagine a man using the name *Pegasus*. It's more likely to be a yacht or something similar. I'd better release the crew and then see if we can prepare a suitable welcome for the big boss."

After a quick search, they found all members of the crew, from the captain down, had been locked in the fo'c'sle. There was no possible way of escape, so with the philosophy of the sailor, they had accepted the situation and made themselves comfortable. They were all asleep when the door was opened, but in seconds, they were wide awake.

Mr. Pallant explained what had happened while they slept and was surprised when several members of the crew insisted on shaking his hand and congratulating him.

"You would have made a good sailor," said the Bo'sun gruffly.

"I used to be one," he chuckled. "Maybe that did make things a little easier!"

Captain Sellers now resumed command. "Mr. Hawtin, take a couple of hands and collect those four men. Stow them in the Bo'sun's locker and leave a guard nearby. Put another man on guard outside the messroom. Don't interfere with men inside though, they are probably armed. Collecting them is a job for the police when we reach port. After that, start heaving the anchor. I want to be away from here before this *Mr. Pegasus* arrives. We've had enough trouble for one night."

"Aye-aye, sir," replied the mate. Selecting two of the younger members of the crew he led them aft, while the rest of the men went to their usual stations to prepare to get under way.

Mrs. Pallant and the girls were still on the poop deck when her husband and the captain returned aft. It was now the darkest hour before dawn and the world seemed very still. They were all discussing the exciting events of the past few hours when Pauline happened to glance astern. Her eyes widened and she clutched her mother's arm.

"Look!" she exclaimed in a voice that was barely a squeak. "The ghostship!"

The others immediately stopped talking and stared at her. Then they all swung around to follow her pointing finger. They saw only blackness.

"Pauline!" said her father reprovingly. "This is no time for jokes."

"But I saw it," she insisted. "A sailing ship with square sails that were kind of glowing."

"That's right!" exclaimed Wendy. "I see it now, too."

As they all watched in fascination as a two masted square rigger seemed to emerge from the surrounding blackness. It was never more than a faint glow and it soon began to fade again. There were no navigation lights showing, nor any sign of life, and the decks seemed to be shrouded in some kind of mist.

Suddenly, a reddish flare appeared forward, only to disappear quickly, apparently taking the ship with it because, once again, they found themselves staring into darkness.

"That must be the ghost ship that Anita was telling us about!" Wendy sounded half excited, half scared.

"Well, I never thought to see the day when—" began Captain Sellers, but he was interrupted by a deep voice from the other side of the deck.

"Freeze! Everybody face this way and raise your hands above your heads!"

With a sharp intake of breath, they all swung around and were able to make out two dark figures on the outside of the far rail.

Apparently, two men had climbed quietly onboard while they were all watching the ghost ship.

The men vaulted over the rail and landed lightly on deck and began approaching.

Soon, they were all close enough for the others to see that each carried a revolver.

*Bertram Smith*

# Chapter Twenty

## *PEGASUS.*

"Stand still, everybody," ordered one of the men. Then, calling over his shoulder, he said: "Send the signal, Sam."

There came the rapid chatter of a signal lamp, during which time, Captain Sellers was able to recover his wits. "What is the meaning of this?" he demanded, stepping forward. "I am the master of this ship and I—"

"Good!" interrupted the intruder. "You are just the man I want to see. I am Sergeant Foster of the Royal Canadian Mounted Police, and I would like to know who owns this big motorboat you have tied up alongside. Also, why an S.O.S. message was flashed from here a few hours ago."

"I sent the message," put in Harry quickly.

All eyes turned to him, but it was Pete who spoke up. "Oh, we forgot to mention that. We heard an aeroplane coming towards the ship and Harry thought of sending an S.O.S. by flashlight through the porthole. We didn't think it had been noticed."

"Oh, it was noticed, all right," said the sergeant. "It was a good idea and it gave us the perfect excuse to board this ship. And now, tell us about the boat alongside, Captain."

"I don't know who owns the boat," began Captain Sellers, "but the men on it held us at gunpoint – just as you are doing."

As he spoke, two more dark figures vaulted lightly over the rail behind the sergeant.

"Signal acknowledged," reported one. "They will be here in a few minutes."

"Very good," responded the sergeant. "Now, Captain, what happened to those men whom, you say, held you up at gunpoint?"

"Safe under lock and key, thanks to these people," the captain gave a brief outline of how his passengers came to be on board and the behavior of the gangsters before being captured.

As he was doing so, the red, white, and green navigation lights of a motorboat came into view, and soon, a sleek police launch slid alongside.

"This is our patrol boat," explained the policeman, as he returned his revolver to his holster. "I decided to use a fishing boat and these clothes to be sure of getting close without arousing suspicion." Turning to his companion, he said: "Sam, you and the others collect this gang. Be careful of the two in the messroom. They might try to shoot it out. The mate will show you where they are."

As his men left, he went to the ship's rail and called down to the patrol boat. "All clear, you can come up now."

A slim figure wearing a blue reefer jacket and a fisherman's woolen cap swung lightly onboard.

"Are they all right?" asked a concerned, unmistakable female voice.

*"Anita!"* exclaimed five voices at once. "What on earth are you doing here?" exclaimed Mrs. Pallant, recovering her wits first, running into an embrace with her first-born daughter.

Anita laughed as she threw her arms around her mother. "I might ask you the same question! Since when has my family been mixed up with international crooks?"

"But—" her father began.

"I'll tell you about it later—once I hear your story," she interrupted. "The sergeant was good enough to let me come along, and I don't want to hold him up."

"Right!" said the policeman. "Now, I need a lot more details from the captain."

He soon found out that the captain did not know many of the details so they had to be filled in by Mr. Pallant and the four youngsters. When the four were called upon though, they all started talking at once and interrupting one another.

Finally, the sergeant held up a large hand. "Whoa! I suggest you elect a spokesman, or we'll be here all day!"

Now they all seemed tongue-tied, with no spokesman at all.

"All right, Pete," said his father at last. "You are usually good at telling stories. Let's have it."

Pete cleared his throat self-consciously and then managed a pretty clear story of the events from the time they were locked in the storeroom until their attempted hold-up of his own father.

Both Anita and the sergeant both had to laugh at this point. "Maybe I should draft you all into the R.C.M.P.!" he joked.

Anita was even more impressed, "What a story!" she exclaimed. "And what a family! You are a real bunch of heroes! I wish now that I had been able to come along and join the fun."

"It wasn't all fun, believe me," put in her mother. "Especially that awful cigar!"

"Well, now you have the full story and the criminals," said Captain Sellers. "I may as well tell you I was about to get under way. I intended to be elsewhere when this *Pegasus* arrived."

The sergeant shook his head. "I'm afraid not, Captain. It is the big boss of this outfit that we are after, and we need your ship to help us trap him."

Captain Sellers hesitated for a moment. "Well, I suppose it is my duty to help the police, so I haven't much choice. What do you need me to do?"

The policeman looked at his watch. "It is past four thirty now, so we haven't much time. I will send our boat away with all the prisoners except the leader. We may be able to use him as a decoy. The finishing boat can go, too. I will stay here with a couple of men and wait for this *Pegasus*, whatever it is. Miss Pallant can stay if she wishes, or the whole family can leave if they are concerned about their safety. There is nothing for you to do, Captain, except stay at anchor and keep everybody out of the way."

"Are you staying, Anita?" asked her father.

"You bet I am!" she chuckled. "I wouldn't miss this for anything!"

"We'll stay, too," put in her mother quietly.

The two men in the messroom had decided to come out quietly when they heard that the R.C.M.P. was on board. Soon all six were on deck looking sullen and dejected. Five were helped over the ship's rail down to the police launch, while Ed, the leader, was returned to the messroom, much to his surprise. He could be heard loudly demanding why he was being separated from the others. No one bothered to reply.

The fishing boat also cast off and things settled down on the *Lulanga*. Except for the big motorboat alongside, she appeared to be an ordinary freighter at anchor. There was nothing to do now except watch and wait, to find out what *Pegasus* might be.

"It's past five o'clock," announced Captain Sellers a little later. "If *Pegasus* is a private yacht, it should be in sight by now. There is nothing heading this way, so maybe the big boss isn't coming after all."

He barely finished speaking when a faint drone was heard.

"An aeroplane!" exclaimed Sergeant Foster. "Of course. *Pegasus* would be something that flies."

The drone grew louder and soon the watchers could make out a plane approaching from the south.

"Maybe it's an ordinary commercial aircraft," said the captain as he focused his big binoculars. "No, it isn't," he added quickly. "It's a flying boat with twin motors."

Before very long, the plane was close enough to see clearly and Pete quickly identified it as a **PBY** Amphibian, a wartime type used mainly for anti-submarine work, but now almost obsolete.

"I guess this must be *Pegasus*," said the sergeant. "I don't know how we are going to trap him though. He will probably be expecting some kind of recognition signal. Everybody out of sight, please."

The flying boat was now reducing height and heading straight for the ship. Gleaming silver in the early light, it made a beautiful picture as it passed low overhead. The roar of the powerful motors echoed thunderously off the ship as it banked and started to circle.

"I'll try to entice him by waving a mooring rope from the stern," said Sergeant Foster. "Sam, bring the prisoner out on deck and keep a close eye on him to make sure he doesn't try any tricks."

Going to the stern of the ship, the sergeant picked up a mooring rope with a loop in the end. This is held high above his head as an invitation to the flying boat to align and tie up to the ship.

The prisoner was marched on deck and warned by a burly constable to do exactly as he was told and no more. The others had crowded under the wing of the bridge from where they could see without being seen.

The flying boat had by now completed its circuit and, turning into wind, it began to lose height rapidly.

"He's almost down," whispered Anita as though afraid of being overheard.

The sea was smooth except for a very light swell and the aircraft made a near-perfect landing. Spray roared up from each side of the hull as it touched the water and then died away as speed was reduced for taxying. As it approached the ship, a hatch in the nose of the flying boat was thrown open and a man appeared with a short boathook, ready to pick up the mooring rope.

There appeared to be scarcely enough room in the hatchway for the torso of one man, but the watchers saw another man squeeze up along the first and train a pair of binoculars on the ship.

Everybody on the *Lulanga* was concentrating on the aircraft when suddenly Ed, the prisoner, made a jump for the ship's rail. He was half over it before the constable caught him, but he had achieved his main objective.

The two men in the nose of the aircraft disappeared quickly and the hatch was slammed. Seconds later, the purr of the motors changed to a roar and the machine began to pick up speed.

"He's taking off again," said Mr. Pallant. "He hasn't left himself much room though."

The flying boat was soon traveling at high speed straight for the ship. The distance between them diminished rapidly until, almost at the last moment, it changed course very slightly and took off. The big machine seemed almost to leap into the air and everybody rushed out to see as it thundered close by at little more than eye level.

"What a take-off!" exclaimed Mr. Pallant. "That pilot knows his job."

"I saw the name clearly," said Anita. "It was *Pegasus*, above a winged horse."

"That's right, great job Anita!" agreed her mother.

The sergeant dropped the mooring rope and walked back to the group. "Lost him!" he said in a disappointed tone. "I did the wrong thing in having that man brought on deck after all. He made a clever move at the right time, though. Take him away, Sam."

The prisoner laughed sardonically. "Now I am sure getting a good lawyer!"

As he was led away, the sergeant commented: "Well, we can't really complain, and neither can the New York Police Department, although it would have been wonderful to catch the big boss. We've made a pretty good haul and probably prevented many more crimes being committed. I'll have a description of that flying boat circulated and we may yet pick him up. Another plus, as far as I am concerned is that our ghost ship trick worked again."

There was silence for a moment as the others tried to understand.

Finally, the skipper spoke up. "You mean that ghost ship was some kind of trick?"

The policeman smiled happily. "I'm glad to be able to say that it was! During the last year or so, we have been plagued by smugglers in this area. They operate at night with boats much faster than ours, so we have been helpless. Then my chief suggested that if we could somehow take advantage of the local legend about a ghost ship appearing occasionally, we might be able to distract the smugglers long enough to trap them. Of course, it can be used only on moonless nights, but that happens to be when smugglers prefer to operate!"

"We've been able to try it only once before, but it worked just fine and we caught half a dozen smugglers in the act. It seemed to work pretty good tonight too, because we were able to board this ship without being seen."

"You were indeed," agreed Captain Sellers. "That thing certainly held our attention."

"Oh, dear!" said Wendy. "What a disappointment. I was sure it was a real ghost ship. You should have seen it, Anita! It looked really scary!"

"I did see it!" her sister chuckled. "I wasn't very far away, you know. I'm so glad you thought it was the real thing, because I helped to design the whole thing!"

The others were all looking at Anita in stunned disbelief.

"That's true," nodded the sergeant. "We couldn't have done it without Anita's expertise."

"How could anyone possibly design a ghost ship?" asked her mother at last, in awe of her first born.

"It was a real challenge," Anita admitted. "Sergeant Foster arranged for a small square-rigged training ship and a little tug to be hired. The tug was lashed alongside, on the side away from the viewers, so that the ship could be moved slowly forward, even against the wind."

"That was the easy part," put in the sergeant. "We still had to make the ship look ghostly. Knowing that Anita was an artist, I asked her if she had any ideas for this very secret project. She certainly did, and pretty quickly!"

"It was my idea to use smoke bombs to make the decks look hazy," went on Anita. "And then I had the sergeant run wiring up and down the rigging and use low power electric bulbs to faintly illuminate the sails from both sides. The power was from batteries carried on the tug. I was able to help by designing a pattern for the lights to go from low to dim at varying intervals. Then, by using a few colored bulbs, we managed a really mysterious, peculiar, ghostly effect."

"Just like dressing a Christmas tree," chuckled Sergeant Foster, obviously well satisfied with her pet project.

The four had been regarding Anita with something approaching awe when her father spoke up. "Absolutely brilliant, Anita! I didn't know we had such brains along with the beauty in the family."

"Of course we have!" her mother beamed with pride.

"I'm so very, very proud of you, Anita," her father hugged her tightly. "You really saved the day!"

Captain Sellers had been as interested a listener as any of the others, but he had his ship to think about. "What happens now, Sergeant?" he asked.

"Well, now. As soon as our patrol boat returns, we'll take the prisoner away, and we may as well tow his boat into Halifax with us. That is, unless you are bound for there."

"I am indeed," replied the captain. "And I'll be glad to bring it along for you."

"Halifax!" exclaimed Anita. "That's where I live. And these people are visiting me. Would it be possible for all of us to stay onboard and go back with you?"

The captain agreed wholeheartedly. "After what they've done for us, they are welcome to the run of my ship at any time!"

"Wow!" exclaimed Harry. "I've always wanted a trip on a freighter."

"Me too!" put in Pete. "I'd like to take a look around the whole ship."

"That might be interesting," said Wendy. "In daylight, that is."

"Yeah!" agreed Pauline. "Especially the places which were so dark last night when we had our adventures."

"That can easily be arranged," smiled the captain. "As soon as the sergeant has gone and we are under way.

"Before you go, sergeant," said the skipper. "I would like to find out what is behind all of this. We have lost our boat and came close to losing our lives, but I still can't see any reasons for it."

"I know how you feel," responded the policeman. "I intend to stress in my report that you and your family were responsible for the capture of these criminals, and I will certainly mention your boat being lost in the process."

He paused for a moment and then added: "There is a lot I don't understand about this case, too. I wonder if the prisoner would be willing to give us any information. Let's all go to the messroom and I'll have him brought in. Maybe he will be willing to co-operate."

The messroom was not much bigger than the galley next door, to which it was connected by a serving hatch in one bulkhead. A large table in the center left only just enough room for ten chairs and two settees.

As soon as everyone was seated, Ed, the gangster was ushered in. He sat down at one end of the table and for the first time the others were able to get a close look at his face. It was hard, with cold eyes, and the four were fascinated.

"A real live gangster!" breathed Wendy.

"Probably a killer!" added Pauline.

The two boys exchanged glances, apparently sharing the same thought: These men looked much more dangerous in daylight than they had in the dark shadows during the night.

The gangster looked carefully around the table. "What's this?" he demanded harshly. "A trial?" his voice had a strong New York accent.

"Not at all," replied Sergeant Foster. "We merely want some information. In half an hour or so, I am going to take you to Halifax and there you will be given the opportunity to make a statement which will be taken down. You are under no obligation to make one now, or say anything at all. However, these people have lost their boat and had a rough time, one way or another, and naturally they are curious to know what it is all about. Would you care to satisfy their curiosity? I assure you that anything you say will be off the record."

The man thought for a moment and then shrugged his shoulders.

"I don't suppose we'll gain anything by trying to hide the reason we came here," he began. "This is the first time we've ever operated outside New York, and so far as I'm concerned, it's the last. If I can have a smoke, I'll tell you the whole story."

The officer handed him a cigarette and he lit it, slowly taking a puff, making the ending embers glow.

He slowly looked around the table, catching each person's eye.

*Bertram Smith*

# Chapter Twenty-One

## *THE GANGSTER'S STORY.*

The sergeant passed him a cigarette, and Ed began: "We've been pretty busy lately, and things began to get too hot for us in New York, so the boss decided we should lay low for a while. He happened to read in a newspaper one day that two engineers were digging for treasure supposed to be worth several million dollars on Oak Island. They seemed sure they would reach it within a couple of weeks and it occurred to him that this could be worth looking into. It might also provide a good hide-out for us, so he sent a man up to investigate.

"Jake Hill went, and he was lucky enough to get a temporary job helping the treasure hunters. He reported that they apparently knew what they were doing and were confident of success. So, the Boss sent the rest of us along in his yacht – a converted Navy Torpedo Boat. We had orders to stay in the vicinity of the island until Jake let us know that the treasure had been found. Then we were to move quickly, hi-jack it, and head for a prearranged meeting place where the boss would pick it up with *Pegasus.* It seemed like a good plan, but, as you know, it didn't work out."

There was a short silence as the listeners digested their story. Then the skipper asked: "Was it you who cut our boat adrift in the small lagoon?"

"Yes, we saw the mastheads through the trees and went in to investigate. We thought you had probably gone ashore to snoop around the treasure, which we expected would be found very soon, and we decided that in case you had any ideas similar to our own, it would be wise to remove your boat. We could hardly believe it when we saw you sailing quietly along next day as though nothing had happened. How did you get your boat back?"

"Luckily for us, it drifted back," Mr. Pallant replied. "I still don't see why you had to charge at our boat like you did, and there was no reason to start shooting, you almost killed me."

"That was Charlie. He's captain of the boat and responsible for her. We were all thoroughly bored after cruising around that island for ten days and we thought we'd have a little fun charging as close to you as possible, and maybe scare you off at the same time. We would have left a few minutes later if it hadn't been for that rope around our propellors. When Charlie realised what happened, and the thought of having to explain a big repair bill to the big Boss, he went berserk and grabbed the rifle. He managed to start firing before we could grab him and put a stop to it."

"But why worry about people sailing near the island?" asked Sergeant Foster. "How could they affect your plans?"

The gangster shrugged. "The boss always had a suspicious mind and I suppose he figured that if he had plans to hi-jack the treasure, other people might have too. Which, of course is quite possible."

"Quite a story," commented the sergeant. "I certainly would like to meet your Boss. Does he use that flying boat all the time?"

"That is something I don't have to talk about."

"No, I suppose not. We heard rumors that he has a secret hideaway in the Caribbean. Well, I think that takes care of everything. I imagine the people who are going to be most surprised are those engineers who are searching for the treasure. I will call and see them on the way to Halifax. It should be interesting to see their reaction when they hear that six people were down below near the treasure when they blew it up, and another six waiting to hi-jack it if their efforts were successful."

"Can I ask a question?" queried the gangster

"Go ahead."

"How did the R.C.M.P. get involved in all of this?"

"I think we'd all like to hear that," put in Captain Sellers, and there was a general murmur of agreement around the table.

"Simple enough," said the sergeant. "The New York Police Department warned us some time ago that some of their most-wanted crooks might be moving up to Canada for a while because of the constant pressure being put on them. Then we received reports that a big motorboat was cruising near Oak Island and warning yachtsmen to keep away. One of our planes was sent to investigate and the pilot reported that the boat looked like a converted Navy Torpedo Boat and it could probably outrun any of our police boats.

"Knowing about the treasure hunt, we guessed what might be happening, and I was put in charge of the case. I could have asked for a Navy Destroyer to be sent after the boat, but I realised that might only result in the boat being chased away temporarily, leaving it free to return any time without us knowing.

"So I decided to have the plane carry out a daily reconnaissance and, when the time came, I would try to get in close with a fishing boat. Our patrol boat would stand by out of sight, and our ghost ship might also be brought along. This could be a good opportunity to use it because such men were almost sure to be armed and we would need something to distract their attention.

"However, we were well on our way from Halifax when the plane reported that the M.T.B. was now tied up alongside a small steamer and also that an S.O.S. message had been received from the ship.

"This was an unexpected development. If the steamer was some kind of mother ship, we might have more men to deal with than we had anticipated. However, it was too late to change our plans, so we came on and found that most of our work had been done for us, thanks to this brave family!"

Half an hour later, the police boat pulled away from the *Lulanga* while Captain Sellers and his guests lined the rail to wave goodbye. The captain was in a jovial mood.

"I've never known anything like this in thirty years at sea," he remarked. "This is certainly the most interesting voyage I've ever made, and I want to thank you people for the part that you played. If you had not been onboard, things might have turned out very different. Please consider yourselves my guests, with the freedom of my ship until we reach Halifax."

Harry's face lit up. "What shall we do first?" he asked of nobody in particular.

"I think what we all need first is a rest," said his aunt.

"A rest?" Pete sounded horrified. "Why, I want to see everything. I've never been on a ship before."

"Me too," echoed Pauline.

But Wendy was silent. She was standing with a puzzled frown on her face. "I've just remembered that I haven't seen Pip since we came on board, and with all of the excitement, I'm afraid I forgot about him. Where is he, I wonder?"

Captain Sellers laughed. "Don't worry about your little dog. He made friends with our cat and shared his food and also his bed in the crew's quarters. He was locked up with us, but he didn't seem to mind. When you released us, I saw him wander outside, take a look around and then go back inside."

Wendy sighed with relief and then chuckled: "I know him. When he saw that it was still dark, he went back to bed!"

The mate, Jeffrey, appeared with Pip in tow and reported that everything was ready to get the ship underway.

"Thank you, Jeff," replied the captain. "We are going right now. Make sure the motorboat is secure: we are taking it to Halifax. Then heave in the anchor. I'll see you people later," he added as he turned towards the bridge.

The voyage to Halifax proved to be a memorable one for the four. They were allowed to go everywhere, and the boys took a hand in everything they possibly could. The girls were not quite so keen on peering into odd places, so when Harry suggested that they all go down below to see the stokehold,

Pauline wrinkled her nose and said, "It's hot and smelly down there. I prefer to act like a passenger and lounge in the sun. What do you think, Wendy?"

"I think you're right. Boys seem to like smelly places for some reason. Come along,. Pip, let's go do some lounging."

"We can sit in the sun at home," observed her brother as the two boys headed for the familiar doorway with the tool rack just inside. Soon, they were descending a slippery, vertical steel ladder. This led to a steel grille platform half way down and they paused to take a look around. From here, they could see the whole engine room. Everything seemed to be moving, clacking, and hissing in an atmosphere heavy with steam and oil.

A similar ladder took them down to the lowest level, far below the waterline. This was decked with steel plating which, like the ladders and all the machinery, gleamed with a thin film of oil. The air was very warm and humid and filled with noise – a rhythmic pulsing clamor which made ordinary speech impossible.

The Second Engineer, a cheerful young man, was on duty and he gladly explained the operation of the big steam engine as well as the various pumps and generators, although he had to raise his voice to do so. The forward part of the engine room was completely filled by two huge boilers, and the boys could feel the heat being thrown back from them.

"Where is the stokehold?" asked Harry in a loud voice.

"Through there," the engineer pointed to a narrow passage between the boilers and waved them on. Harry led the way through the short, dark passage into increasing heat. Two men were busy with shovels, one transferring coal from a side bunker while the other was preparing to feed a furnace. He swung open the furnace door and the boys felt a blast of heat which made them draw back quickly.

Although much hotter, it was not so noisy in this small hold and conversation was a little easier. The man feeding the furnace was a lean red-head who, after slamming one furnace door, quickly opened t'other. Then, holding out his shovel, he said: "Want to try it?"

"Sure," said Pete, grabbing it quickly. He was surprised at the weight of the shovel itself, and even more so when he tried to lift it full of coal. With a grunt, he reduced it to half a load and swung it towards the gaping furnace.

Only then did he notice that the slight roll of the ship was enough to deflect his aim. The coal splattered against the front of the boiler with only a few pieces actually entering the furnace.

The other man had stopped work to watch and he joined in the laughter as Pete stared in surprise. A second attempt was more successful, and then Harry had to try. He soon showed that his farm experience with a shovel made a big difference, and having seen Pete's mistake, he allowed for the deviation and shot his coal deep into the furnace, causing it to give a raucous roar. Quickly, the stoker slammed the door shut.

"A change from treasure hunting!" Harry said with a grin.

"It sure is," agreed Pete. "A lot warmer, too!"

"Where did you stash it?" asked the other man, who had now drawn close.

"Stash what?" Pete was taken by surprise and Harry looked equally puzzled.

"The treasure. We heard you found over ten million dollars in gold and jewelry!"

Both boys burst out laughing while Harry explained how they had missed out on the treasure hunting. The two men exchanged glances and then looked suspiciously at the boys. Apparently satisfied with what they saw, they appeared to accept the story.

"Ah, well," said the red-head. "So much for rumors!"

# Chapter Twenty-Two

## *GREAT NEWS!*

Back on deck, the boys breathed deeply of the clean air. "I don't think I would like to be a stoker," said Pete.

"Nor me," said his cousin. "Not even a marine engineer. I am too fond of fresh air."

They found the girls spread out on the poop enjoying the sun, with Pip in his back between them. As they were describing what it was like down below, the skipper strolled into view.

"What happened to your mother and Anita?" he asked.

"There they are," said Pauline, who happened to be facing the correct way. "Just coming down from the bridge."

"And looking very pleased with themselves," observed her father. "What have you two been up to?" he asked as mother and daughter drew near.

"We've been doing a little organising," answered Mrs. Pallant with a smile.

"Mother has," corrected Anita. "I only wish I could be a part of it."

Her sisters sat up, and everybody except Pip was suddenly very interested.

"Tell us!" insisted Pauline after waiting a moment.

Her mother looked around at them all. "The captain invited us up on the bridge and we had a very interesting time. He is such a nice man. Did you know this ship is a tramp steamer and spends most of its time calling at ports in Nova Scotia and Maine?" she asked her husband.

He shook his head. "Although I could probably have guessed. Why do you ask?"

"Well, naturally I asked him if he ever goes into Portland and he told me he expects to be there in a couple of weeks! So I explained how our vacation has been interrupted, ruined in fact, and asked him if it would be possible for us to stay on board until we reach home. He said we would be very welcome to do so!"

"Whoopee!" exclaimed Pete. "Now we can relax and enjoy ourselves."

"He has half a dozen calls to make before Portland," put in Anita. "So, you will be able to go sightseeing at some strange ports. He is behind schedule now though, so the ship will be staying in Halifax for only a few hours and leaving again tonight. You probably won't even have time to come home with me. I sure wish I could stay on board for a couple of weeks too."

The *Lulanga* reached Halifax in the afternoon, and the guests were all invited onto the bridge as she entered port.

"A little different from the first time we arrived here," commented the skipper. "But it's all been a very interesting experience."

"I think it's been an exciting adventure!" declared Harry. "I know my dad will be green with envy when I tell him all about it!"

"Why not write him a long letter?" grinned Anita. "Then your father can begin being envious all the sooner?"

"Good idea!" said the boy. "I'll do that tomorrow."

Now the ship was entering the inner harbor and they all watched with keen interest as Captain Sellers carefully maneuvered his vessel alongside the quay with scarcely a bump.

Immediately the mooring lines were made fast, a gang of stevedores clambered on board and started opening the hatches. Soon, steam winches were clanking and hissing, while derricks swung cargo up out of the hold and ashore.

It was a noisy and apparently confused scene which made Harry comment, "Gee! All this makes life on a farm seem peaceful and quiet."

"Well, I had better be going," said Anita. "My boss will be wondering what has happened to me. At least I don't have much packing to do." She looked a little tearful as she hugged each one in turn. "I sure wish I was going along with you. Please don't have any more adventures without calling me in first! I really enjoyed sharing that one with you all."

"You will surely be missed most of all, Anita!" her mother hugged her tightly. The others all rejoiced once more at Anita saving the day with her incredible art skills on the ghost ship details. Everyone waved enthusiastically as she walked down the plank.

The din and the shouting fell as dusk fell, and the *Lulanga* got under way again. Now the guests were able to see a very different scene as the ship moved slowly passed dimly lighted quays with their huge sheds for sorting cargo. Other vessels were alongside, some working cargo under bright cluster lights.

"Things sure do look bigger in the dark," commented Pauline. "Even the ships look bigger."

During the next two weeks, the *Lulanga* called at a different port every day or two, so there was never any reason for boredom. The four took the opportunity to explore each small port for an hour or two, and all kept careful diaries – or log books, as Pete now preferred to call them.

While at sea, they managed to explore almost every corner of the ship, much to the amusement of the crew. Even Pip seemed to become accustomed to life on a ship.

Mr. and Mrs. Pallant took the opportunity to relax, usually on the open poop deck.

One day, the four were with them, wondering if there was anything else to do on the ship when Wendy had an idea. "There is one more thing I'd like to do on this ship, and that is to take the wheel. It would be very interesting to see how different it is from steering the *Seawolf.*"

"You won't find it very exciting," remarked her father. "In fact, it can be downright boring. However, if you ask the captain, I think he might give you permission."

"If it's boring," said Pete, "It's not for me."

Harry thought for a moment. "Me too," he decided.

"I'll come too! I love our sister mini-adventures," cheered Pauline.

The girls went off to find the captain and were fortunate enough to meet him on deck. Hesitatingly, Wendy asked if it would be possible for them to try their hands at steering the ship.

"Why not?" smiled Captain Sellers. "You kids seem to have done just about everything else onboard! Come along. I am just about to relieve the officer of the watch for a while."

The bridge was open and stretched from one side of the ship to the other. An expanse of spotless teak deck broken only by the binnacle and the wheel exactly in the center and in line with the keel. The helmsman, a burly seaman with a skin like leather, grinned when he was told to teach these two faire sea-maidens how to steer.

Standing to one side, he made room for Pauline to take the first turn. And began to explain about the compass and how the mark inside the binnacle was called a lubber line, which indicated the course the ship was actually on.

Pauline could only just see down into the huge brass binnacle enclosing the compass, but she gave a wheel a tentative turn to see what would happen. Nothing did, and she peered closer at the black lubber line. It was not moving either.

"Watch her head," cautioned the seaman. "You'll see movement there before you'll see it on the compass. There, look at her now," he added, pointing ahead. Pauline looked up just in time to see a ship in the far distance move quickly across from the port bow to the starboard bow as the *Lulanga* started to swing.

"Meet her," called the captain from the bridge wing.

Pauline and Wendy were at a loss.

"Turn the wheel the other way," the seaman urged, and the girl hurriedly obeyed.

"Now you're meeting her," said the captain as he strolled over.

Just as he spoke, Pauline felt a strong vibration under her feet which made the deck shake, and she could not help but to look down in alarm. Wendy felt it too, and looked puzzled.

"That is the steam steering the engine in the deckhouse just below," explained the captain. "It is old, like the ship, and doesn't respond as quickly as it should. Then, once it does, it is difficult to stop, by which case, the ship is usually off course. Take a look at your wake."

Pauline looked over her shoulder and gasped when she saw the usually arrow-straight wake looking like an elongated letter 'S'.

Captain Sellers laughed at her consternation. "Not to worry!" he said. "It just so happens that this is a difficult ship to steer until you get used to it. If you try giving her only a little helm and then waiting, you will do it all right. I imagine it is a little different from steering the schooner, though, eh?"

"It certainly is!" agreed Pauline. "The *Seawolf* feels the lightest touch on the wheel. Doesn't she, Wendy?"

"She does, indeed. Let me try this one," agreed Wendy.

Pauline was not unwilling to hand over this unwieldy ship which seemed to have a mind of its own and she watched gleefully as her sister started to wrestle with the noisy but invisible steering mechanism. Wendy found it no easier, even though she knew the reason for the problem. She soon realised that she was not likely to produce a straight wake soon, so after a good try, she was glad to let the regular helmsman take over.

Returning to the poop, they were greeted by the skipper with a mischievous gleam in his eye. "What happened to the man at the wheel?" he asked. "The ship seems to be out of control!"

"That was Pauline steering," chuckled Wendy. "Me too, a little."

"Oh, I thought the maybe the man had collapsed on duty!"

"Well, the steering engine is old and worn," said Pauline defensively. "Even the captain says this is a very difficult ship to steer."

"Excuses, excuses!" yawned Pete.

Now the skipper was really interested. "A worn steering engine, eh? I was on a ship which had one once and it was a challenge to steer at all. The steering engine was old, and the parts so worn and loose that by the time I got it around to moving the rudder, the ship was way off course. Steering was a constant battle; no dozing at the wheel with her. I'm so proud of you girls for giving it all you've got."

All too soon they were informed that the next port of call would be Portland.

"What a pity," sighed Mrs. Pallant. "I was just getting used to the life of leisure!"

"It's a shame we couldn't take the *Seawolf* back with us," said Wendy. "But it sure will be nice to see the old house again."

Soon, the familiar skyline appeared, and all too quickly the ship was being warped alongside the dock. The gangway clanged into position, and suddenly it was time to say goodbye to the ship's crew. As an indication of their popularity, every member insisted on shaking hands, and Captain Sellers cheerfully waited his turn.

"This has been a very pleasant association," he declared. "You are welcome to sail with me again at any time."

"Thank you, Captain," replied Mr. Pallant. "We've enjoyed ourselves and your offer is appreciated. I hope that one day we may be able to take you up on it."

"Come along, Pip," said Wendy, hobbling along with that pesky rock still in her shoe. "We are going to our very own home."

As the family walked down the gangway, they heard a sailor whistle to them, and they all turned back to see the captain and crew all lined up against the railing with full salute. The family chuckled and each returned the respectful gesture.

Fifteen minutes later, they had squeezed into the car and were on their way home at last.

"It seems as though we've been away for months instead of weeks," Pete remarked as their house came into view. "And the old house ought to look different somehow."

Pip went wild with delight at seeing his own private backyard again and rushed around sniffing everywhere.

The four had similar, if more subdued, feelings about their rooms, but it did not take them long to settle back into their old routine.

"Well, that really was an adventure," observed Pauline as they sprawled on the beach the next day.

"I'm just glad to finally be wearing a different pair of shoes! I never could get that rock out of my adventure shoe," Wendy rejoiced.

"What a pity it's over," agreed Pete.

But it was not quite over, as they found a couple of days later when a letter arrived for Mr. Pallant from Sergeant Foster. They decided to all read it out in the garden on this bright sunny day:

*Dearest Mr. and Mrs. Pallant and family,*

*I am sure you will be interested to know that Pegasus was traced to a secret hide-out by the U.S. Coastguard. They captured several more well-known criminals, including the leader, and also recovered most of the proceeds of that big bank robbery that we heard had taken place in New York City.*

*The bank concerned had offered a substantial reward for the recovery of the money, and this is being divided among the various people who helped in the operation. I am directed by the Commissioner to inform you that your share of the reward will likely be several thousand dollars. When the exact amount is known, a check will be forwarded to you.*

*Congratulations, good luck, and I hope we meet again.*

*Warmest regards, Sergeant Foster*

The news brought a stunned silence. "Isn't that wonderful?" the skipper asked at last. "With a little luck, it might work out to about a thousand dollars each!"

Harry was the first to recover his wits. "Thank you, Uncle, but I don't think I should take a share."

"Of course you will," put in his aunt. "No one earned a share more than you did. Anita will have a share, too, of course. I must write and give her the good news. She will be thrilled."

"What are you going to do with your share, Dad?" asked Pete.

"Hmmm. I think I'll put mine towards a new *Seawolf*. The insurance money won't be enough, and I would like a slightly bigger boat."

"Then my share goes towards a bigger boat," said Pete firmly.

"And mine!" exclaimed Pauline.

"Mine too!" exclaimed Wendy.

Her mother smiled at all of the enthusiasm. "Well, there are lots of things I need for the house, but a boat is a family project which keeps us together. So you can please include my share."

"Can I put in my share too?" asked Harry quietly.

"If your parents agree, you are more than welcome to become a partner in the new *Seawolf*, Harry," replied his uncle.

"I feel that if I do, I would absolutely be guaranteeing more adventures!" said the boy happily.

Pete looked around at the others and then said with a sly grin, "This is what I would call a magnificent culmination to a superlative adventure!"

Pauline rolled her eyes in pretend agony. "Oh no! I forgot he had another dictionary at home!" Everybody chuckled.

Mrs. Pallant had been cleaning out all of the children's laundry, and headed back in to continue, only moments later to return, holding Wendy's shoe, her face in shock.

"Ivy, what is it?" Mr. Pallant stood up to go to her.

"Mom, what are you doing with my shoe?" Wendy asked confused.

"I was cleaning all of our adventure clothes, and I remember you'd said you felt like you had a rock in your shoe a couple of times..." she was stunned.

"Yes, Mom..." Wendy guided her to continue.

"I could see the rubber had split at the side, a small hole had formed. Then I felt a large lump on the inside bottom of your shoe, and—" she put her hand to her heart and took a deep breath.

"Yes, Auntie, please tell us!" Harry interrupted.

Everybody gathered around Mrs. Pallant to see what was going on.

She continued, "I peeled back the bottom layer of your shoe lining, and—just look!" she opened up her hand, showing a giant deep blue gemstone, about the size of a toy marble.

"A sapphire!" exclaimed Pauline. "As blue as your eyes, Wendy!"

"This is no sapphire..." Mrs. Pallant exclaimed, breathlessly. "This is the rarest gemstone in the entire world—a blue diamond! Exactly like the Hope Diamond from the Crown Jewels of the Queen of England herself!"

A giant, rare blue diamond gemstone from the massive explosion of the treasure in the murky tunnels on Oak Island. It had scratched Wendy's leg and torn a hole into her shoe, where it had, uncomfortably, remained under the lining until it was ready to present itself to the world.

Each family member was absolutely astonished.

Suddenly, each person let out a loud whoop, holler, and cheer!

Mr. Pallant hoisted Wendy onto his shoulders and danced around excitedly. The family all jumped around in excitement, with Pip running between their feet, barking and wagging his tail enthusiastically, enjoying the elated mood from everybody.

"Hip, hip, hoorah for Wendy's stinky shoe!" Pete started the chant.

"Hip, hip, hoorah! Hip, hip, hoorah!" Everybody chanted along, while Wendy giggled, bouncing atop her father's shoulders.

Mrs. Pallant stopped short, simply staring at the blue diamond in the palm of her hand. "It's so large... it must be worth *one million dollars!* Surely, dear, we cannot keep this."

Mr. Pallant let Wendy down. "You're right, of course. Let me make a phone call."

"You can't be serious, Dad!" Pete cried out.

"It's the right thing to do," his father stated.

He got on the telephone to ring the sergeant. After a few more moments, he was on a call with someone else. The four could overhear him talking for ages about their harrowing adventure.

A few moments later, he came back out to the yard and told everybody to gather around.

"I just got off the telephone with first Sergeant Foster, who put me in touch with the owner of the Oak Island treasure hunt exploration. I told him everything we'd been through, including getting trapped in the tunnels, the explosion, the treasure, nearly drowning, losing our boat, the pirates, the blue diamond, everything.

"He was so appreciative that we had seen the treasure with our own eyes and know exactly where it is, we've all been invited back to the island immediately to participate in the excavation of the treasure!"

Mrs. Pallant watched all of the children's jaws drop open at the news.

Mr. Pallant continued with the great news, "We will each be receiving our very own ancient gold coin as a reward! But that's not all, as a proper way to thank all of us, he's going to buy us a new, much bigger *Seawolf!* Plus, we must be shining at our very best, as we are each to be interviewed on the international television news about how our family solved the Secret of Oak Island after one hundred and sixty-five years of mystery!"

"Hip, Hip, Hoorah!" went the boisterous cheer from each one once more.

Pip joined in with his delighted barking and tail wagging.

*Bertram Smith*

TO PAULINE.

# The Smith Family

The Pallant Family was based 100% on the Smith Family. This tale is fiction, but this adventurous family is very real!

Bertram Smith – Born in England in 1911. At just 14 years old, he joined the British Navy. Once grown, deeply in love, Bert asked Ivy, "Marry me and I'll show you the world!" and three days later they were wed. They lived in South Africa, Egypt, Sudan, England, Canada, settling in California, USA.

Ivy Smith – Born in England in 1912, beloved mother of four. Friends to the Egyptian Royal Family with their first-born daughter. Received a letter from the King of England as a welcome to the famous triplets. She helped solve cold cases as a policework volunteer. First-born Anita, with the triplets Wendy, Pauline, Peter.

They shared their lives for over 50 years.

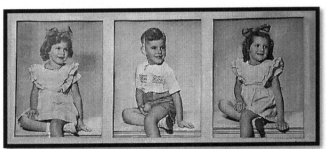

PRIVY PURSE OFFICE,
BUCKINGHAM PALACE.

### THE KING'S BOUNTY.

The Keeper of the Privy Purse has received

His Majesty's commands to pay The King's Bounty to

Mrs.Ivy May Smith, and a cheque for Three pounds is

accordingly forwarded herewith.

11th November,1948.

# Story Beginnings

TWI
CHILDREN WITH INTEGRITY

ENCOURAGING GRANDCHILDREN to read is a lifetime gift. Send for our latest mystery adventure novel–The Secret of Oak Island–for ages 10-15. Satisfaction guaranteed. Send $10 from Herrith Publishing, ███ Belmont, Redondo Beach, CA 90278.

OAK ISLAND.

Courses and distances.

First - 096° (a little south of East) 200 miles
Second- 055 ( NE by East. 130 "
Third 330° ( a little S. of NNW) --20 "
450 ==

3- 4 days hopefully under 3

Average length of chapters in other books
10 pages.

---

**NOTES** FOR OAK ISLAND STORY.

For inside back of dust jacket:

The author is a former sailor adventurer with a knack for spinning
sea yarns laced with humor.

Publicity notice and maybe inside dust jacket (front)

Sail with a modern family into a deadly 17th century pirate trap.

Advert for showcase?

Help your children to break the T.V. habit. Introduce them to
high adventure through reading. An ideal gift for almost any
occasion, The Secret of Oak Island will hold their attention
from cover to cover.

## McCLELLAND AND STEWART LIMITED

Publishers     25 Hollinger Road Toronto 16 Ontario Canada Cables: EMANDESS

April 21, 1964

Mr. Bert Smith,
106 Rosemount Ave.,
Weston, Ontario.

Dear Mr. Smith:

We have now had several readings on your manuscript entitled
THE SECRET OF OAK ISLAND, and regret that, after careful
consideration, we have decided that we will be unable to make a
publishing offer for your work. We appreciate having had this
opportunity to read your manuscript and apologize for not
having given you an earlier decision.

We are returning your manuscript under separate cover by
registered mail and trust it will reach you safely.

Yours sincerely,

McCLELLAND AND STEWART LIMITED

Marian Tilden

Marian Tilden,
Editorial Department.

/mt

Made in the USA
Monee, IL
14 November 2023

46487805R00159